AMISH WIDOW'S DECISION

EXPECTANT AMISH WIDOWS BOOK 15

SAMANTHA PRICE

Faye Kirkdale was cleaning her kitchen while awaiting the arrival of her husband. His evening meal was in the oven keeping warm. Hank always arrived home too late for Faye to wait and eat with him. When she heard the familiar hoofbeats, she poured a glass of his favorite cider and placed it on the table. Faye kept his meal in the oven, knowing it would take him a while to unhitch the buggy and rub down the horse. She sat on the couch and resumed her knitting, waiting for the familiar stomping footfalls up the porch stairs that led to the front door.

After she'd knitted a few rows, she thought it strange that he was still outside. She opened the front door and saw the horse and buggy, not even unhitched.

"Hank!" When there was no reply, she yelled in a louder voice, but still she was met with silence except for the horse snorting in agitation.

She lit one of the gas lanterns and hurried out to see what was happening. Before she reached the horse and buggy, she saw that the horse had his neck up straight and his reins weren't tied to anything. When she got closer, the horse backed away from her, but she managed to lift the lantern high enough to see her husband slumped over in the buggy.

She yelled at Hank, but he didn't move. When she tried to reach for the horse, he reared up and trotted away. All she could do was wait until the horse stopped and then she slowly walked over to him, speaking soft words so he would stay put. There was an eerie feeling about all of this.

"Everything's all right." She continued speaking in a calming voice as she carefully reached over and grabbed the reins and then tied them to a nearby fence post so the horse wouldn't take off again. The horse had been upset by something. Then she stepped over to the buggy and looked at her husband, and gasped when she saw that his white shirt was soaked in blood. She looked closer in case she was wrong. Yes, it was blood. She called out his name. "Hank!" No response. With the lantern in one hand, she felt for a pulse with the other but there was none. "Hank!" she screamed again.

It sank in that he was dead. Her first thought was to call the bishop. She ran into the barn and placed the lantern by her feet. With trembling hands, she picked up the receiver and dialed the bishop's number. She was relieved that she could remember it right now, even though she knew it by heart.

Bishop Luke answered the phone. "Hank's dead!" she screamed into the phone. Then she broke down and sobbed and could barely speak.

"Faye? What's happened?"

She managed to stop crying enough to speak. "He's in the buggy—dead. There's blood all over."

"I'm coming immediately, Faye. Don't do anything. I'll be there soon."

"He came home in the buggy and didn't get out. I went out to see where he was and he's in the buggy covered in blood. He's dead!" Tears rolled down her face.

"Faye, listen to me carefully. Are you alone?"

"*Jah.*"

"Go back into the *haus* and lock the doors. I'll call 911 and then I'll come there. Until then, don't answer the door to anyone unless it's the police or the paramedics."

"Okay."

"Lock yourself in. Do it now."

Without saying anything further, she hung up the receiver, picked up the lantern, and ran into the house. Once she was inside, she obeyed the bishop's words. She made sure the front door was bolted, then she locked the back door, and then she ran around locking all of the windows.

Once she had done that, she looked out the window at the buggy standing still in the darkness. Had someone killed her husband or had some medical problem caused him to bleed so much? She touched her dress and felt it was wet. When she looked down, she saw she was covered in blood. Knowing that the bishop and the paramedics were on the way, she hurried to the mudroom at the back of the house and stripped off her clothes. She washed her hands, then wrapped herself in a towel and hurried upstairs to find clean clothes.

As she grabbed the first dress she came to, a chill shuddered through her body. What if Hank had been murdered right outside her house? What if the murderer had slipped into the house while she'd been on the phone? Or had Hank been murdered elsewhere, and then the horse found its way home?

She made her way back downstairs and sat on the couch. Within minutes, she heard wailing sirens. Jumping to her feet and looking out the window, she saw two police cars and an ambulance pulling into the yard. She opened the door and stepped out of the house.

The paramedics made their way to the buggy with two policemen, and two more policemen walked toward her. "Are you Mrs. Kirkdale?"

"I am." She wiped tears from her eyes. "I found my husband in the buggy. He was dead. He's covered in blood. He was supposed to come in for his dinner." She gasped; she'd forgotten that the dinner was still in the oven. Without saying anything, she turned and rushed to turn off the oven. The two uniformed policemen followed her inside. "I forgot that I hadn't turned off the oven. You see, I was keeping his dinner warm."

"I'm Officer Bryant and this is Officer Carmody."

"I'm Mrs. Kirkdale. Oh, you already know that."

"Yes, we got a call from your bishop. Is he here?"

"No, the only person here is me. And my husband." Just as she was finished saying that, they heard hoofbeats heading toward the house. "That will be the bishop now."

She walked back out of the kitchen to greet the bishop and saw that his wife, Abigail, was there too.

Abigail ran to Faye and put her arms around her. "Oh, you poor thing."

The officers introduced themselves to the bishop and his wife.

"It was horrible." Faye looked back at the police officers who were behind her. "How did he die?"

Rather than answer her question, Officer Bryant said, "We'll soon know. Let's just sit down somewhere and you can tell us exactly what happened."

Tears flooded down her cheeks again. She covered her face with her hands. "I can't say anything at the moment."

"Do you mean you want a lawyer?" Officer Carmody asked.

"I don't want anything at the moment, except to find out what happened to my husband." Suddenly the yard was awash with light. Three battery-operated lights had been erected in her yard. "Was he stabbed? Is that why there was so much blood?"

"We'll talk to the team in a minute."

Her attention was drawn to flashes of light near the buggy. "Are they taking photos?"

"It looks like the buggy is being considered a crime scene," the bishop said to Faye. He asked Officer Carmody, "Is it all right if I look after the horse? He looks like he's been badly spooked, and he might be injured, too."

"Not right now. Maybe in half an hour or so," Officer Carmody said.

The bishop looked a little shocked at the seeming disregard for the animal's well-being, but nodded in agreement.

"Let's sit down."

When they sat down with Officer Bryant, Officer Carmody said, "Mind if I take a look around your house?"

"Yes, yes, do it if you want."

She slumped back into the couch with Abigail on one side of her and the bishop on the other.

"What happened?" asked Officer Bryant. "When did he arrive home?"

"He came home but he didn't come inside. After a while, I went to see what was wrong. I called out to him and there was no answer. I took a light out to check on things, and then I saw him covered in blood and slumped over, almost like he was asleep. I felt for a pulse and couldn't find it. Then I called Bishop Luke."

"And I called 911, and then my wife and I came here," the bishop told him.

Officer Bryant shook his head at the bishop, telling him to keep quiet.

"Can I get you something, Faye?" Abigail asked.

She shook her head. "The only thing I want right now is some answers. Why did this happen?"

Officer Carmody came out of the mudroom with her bloodied clothes hanging from a stick. "Do these look familiar, Mrs. Kirkdale?"

"Yes, I just changed out of them, just now."

"You admit they're your clothes?"

"Yes."

He glanced at them and then looked back at her. "They're covered in blood."

"That's why I changed out of them."

"We're going to need you to come down to the station for questioning," Officer Carmody said.

"Right now?"

"Yes."

She nodded.

"We'll come with you," Abigail said.

"There's no need for that," Officer Bryant said. "We can drive her home when we're finished. It might take some time."

"I'll be fine," Faye said to them. "You go home. I'll call you later."

CHAPTER 2

*J*ust after the bishop and his wife left, Faye was waiting to leave the house for the police station when a different uniformed officer knocked on the door. One of the officers went to the door, and Faye heard the new man say that a paramedic wanted to take a look at her.

The officer turned around. "Mrs. Kirdale ..."

She bounded to her feet, thinking to correct his mispronunciation of her name, and then everything faded into darkness. When she opened her eyes, she was on the floor and someone in white was leaning over her.

"Can you hear me, Mrs. Kirkdale?"

She didn't have the strength to answer. She looked around and realized she must have fainted.

"I can hear you," she whispered weakly.

The paramedic helped her to a seated position. "Easy does it." He took her blood pressure with a portable machine.

"Did I faint?"

"Yes, but it's only normal with the nasty shock you've had." He looked around him and then handed her a couple of loose pills, and said in a low voice, "These will help you sleep."

There was no prescription or anything. She wondered if he was supposed to be handing out sleeping pills like that. "Thank you."

He gave her a reassuring smile. "Physically you're okay. You should go to your local doctor tomorrow. You might need something to get you through the next few days."

She had no intention of going to the doctor. In her mind, going to a doctor was a last resort, and she'd only fainted. "Thanks. I'm okay. The only thing wrong with me is a bee allergy, but …"

"You have an EpiPen?"

"Yes, somewhere."

"Good." He nodded.

"I never had a phone before and when I nearly

died the bishop urged me to get a phone on. Now I'm married the first emergency was for my husband and not for me."

"You'll be okay." He gave her a reassuring smile and she felt embarrassed for rambling about herself when her husband was dead.

AT THE POLICE STATION, Faye gave permission for them to fingerprint her, and then they took her fingerprints as well as photographs of her hands and of both sides of her face. After they were through, they took her into an interview room. There she waited for someone else to interview her.

Faye shivered, and wondered why she was being treated like a criminal. Her husband was dead. She was tired, yet she didn't want to sleep. She was hungry, but didn't want to eat. Faye didn't know what she wanted to do with herself. Closing her eyes in the cold, sterile environment of the room, she asked God why He had taken Hank away from her. Was it because she had prayed once or twice to be set free from the marriage? If that was it, she took it all back. It wasn't the greatest marriage, being wife to the cold and indifferent Hank, but she never wanted him dead. She'd grown used to the life she had and it had brought with it the comfort of routine. Now what would become of her brothers, who relied on Hank's business for employment?

Her parents were the ones who'd wanted her to marry Hank. It hadn't mattered that she didn't love him, not to her parents at least. Their sole reason for her marrying him was to give her younger brothers secure employment.

Long ago, Faye's parents had made a plan, and that plan was that her father would build up a business big enough for their four sons to take over. When her father's legs were crushed in a buggy accident, her parents' plans were crushed right along with them. They then hatched another plan for their sons which involved their oldest child, Faye, marrying the much older Hank. So far, that plan had worked perfectly from her parents' perspective, and each of Faye's brothers had been employed by Hank. No plan had been made for Hank's sudden death. Or had it? She remembered her mother, some time back, asking Hank to make a will. The will left everything to Faye and the children they would have.

Faye jumped when the door was swung open and a tall, broad-shouldered detective walked into the room. He wore a dark suit that didn't fit him very well at the shoulders, and the top three buttons of his shirt were undone, giving him the more casual appearance of someone who didn't particularly like wearing a suit.

When he smiled at her, she immediately relaxed. "Hello, Mrs. Kirkdale. I'm Detective Jed Hervey."

"Hello, Detective. Just call me Faye."

He nodded. "I'm sorry about your husband."

Faye dabbed at the corners of her eyes with a tissue. Her eyes stung because she'd wiped them so much. "Thank you. How did he die?"

"The coroner's trying to ascertain that right now. All we know is that he was stabbed."

Faye sighed. That meant it wasn't a medical condition; someone had taken his life from him.

"Do you have any idea who would want your husband dead?"

"He had no enemies. Everyone liked him. At least, I don't know anyone who didn't. Not enough to kill him, anyway." She shook her head. "Who would do such a thing?"

"Officer Carmody found your clothes in your house, all covered in blood, and one of the officers found a large knife covered in blood by your house."

"I don't know anything about a knife. I told the officers that I changed my clothes because they had blood on them from when I tried to check my husband's pulse." Then Faye remembered something. "I have a knife missing. I used it to cut meat. It was a carving knife with a distinct curved handle. The handle was made from a pale colored wood and it was heavily grained. I looked for it this afternoon when I started fixing dinner, and it wasn't there."

"Wait here a moment." He left and then came back with a cell phone. He showed her a picture on it.

"That's my knife!" It had blood on it, as he'd said.

"That could possibly be the murder weapon."

The detective sat back down then, and clicked on the end of a pen. "What can you tell me about your relationship with your husband?"

"We've been married for four years."

He jotted something down and then looked up at her. "Happily?"

"Adequately." She couldn't lie and say they were happily married. Hank might've been happy, she didn't know, but she wasn't that happy.

He pulled a face. "Adequately?"

She nodded. "I had no cause for complaint."

"How old was your husband?"

"Forty-six."

"And you?"

"Twenty-six."

"That's quite an age difference."

She nodded. "It is. It was."

"And I understand he was a wealthy man and owned a large door-manufacturing business?"

She nodded. "He had a good business. Doors—wooden doors. Sliding doors, French doors, entry doors. They're good quality. Everyone loves them."

"And what will happen to that business now that he's dead? Did your husband have a will?"

"Yes. Everything was left to me and our children. If we had any, that is, but we never did. I can't believe he was stabbed. Who would do that?"

"I can tell you from experience that when someone has been stabbed so many times, there's an emotional element involved. Someone was very upset with him and that's why I asked if he had any enemies."

"You didn't ask if he had enemies. You asked did I know anyone who'd want him dead."

"Did he have any enemies?"

"I can't think of anybody who would be that upset with him."

"What about you?"

She gasped. "You don't think I did this, do you?"

He looked down at the notepaper on the desk and then looked back up at her. "Your dress and apron

17

were covered in blood. The murder occurred on your property, and then there's the knife." He raised his eyebrows as though he was waiting for her to blurt out her confession.

"How do you know he was murdered on my property? It could've happened somewhere—anywhere—on the way home and the horse found his way home."

"You want us to believe that your horse found his way home just like some kind of Lassie?"

"I have no idea what or who a Lassie is, but horses find their way home all the time. When they throw their rider, they find their way home. When a buggy driver falls asleep, they pull the buggy home. Don't you know anything about horses, Detective?"

He leaned back and folded his arms across his chest. "The forensic team will be able to ascertain whether it happened on your property or along the route from his place of business to your house. Now tell me, Mrs. Kirkdale, do you have any reason to want your husband dead?"

"No! Of course not!" She was getting frustrated by answering the same question over and over.

"If you tell us now, things will go easier for you. Did he beat you, and you got angry with him?"

She shook her head. "No, never."

"Was he verbally, emotionally, or physically abusive to you?"

"Never. Not once. He was a good man."

"I know the Amish way of life can be a harsh one. I also know the only way out of marriage, since you folk don't believe in divorce, is death. Did you want out of the marriage?" The officer's brown eyes bored through hers.

She would've loved to have gotten out of the marriage. "I thought about it at times, but that would never happen. Marriage is for life and I knew that when I married him. I didn't kill him. It never entered my head. I could never harm anyone."

"Maybe you got tired of being dominated by a man and wanted your freedom back, and the only way out for an Amish woman is if her husband dies, isn't that right?"

He was repeating himself but she wasn't going to antagonize him by pointing that out. "If you mean the only way she can be free to marry again is if her husband dies, then that is correct. We Amish do allow a husband and wife to live separately if they cannot be compatible in the same house, but there is no divorce."

"Do you want to marry someone else?"

"No! I didn't kill him. I would never kill him. And I don't want to marry someone else."

"You have blood on your hands, literally, and you had blood all over your clothes. He was stabbed viciously and repeatedly and I'm afraid you are our only suspect."

"You'd better find another one soon, because I didn't do it. You should try to find out who did this so it doesn't happen to someone else."

"Would you like to talk to a lawyer?"

"I don't have one. They asked me that before, a couple of times, and I said no. I have nothing to hide because I didn't do it. You're wasting your time with these questions."

"You could find a lawyer. Was it self-defense?"

She pushed out her chair and stood up. "No. Am I free to go?"

"Don't get upset. We're only asking questions that we need to ask."

"I understand, but am I free to go?"

"Yes, but we'll want to talk to you again."

"Where is my husband now?"

"An autopsy is being performed as we speak."

"Where?"

"At the hospital."

"I'd like to see him."

He shook his head. "I'm afraid that's not possible right now. We'll let you know when he's ready to be collected by a funeral director."

She'd already given them the number of her phone in the barn, and the bishop's number.

"We'll be in touch." He reached into his pocket and pulled out a card. "If you remember anything else, or can think of anyone who might have had reason to cause him harm, please call me."

She took the card from him. "Thank you."

"I'll have someone take you home. We'll have officers patrolling your home for the next few days and nights, so don't be nervous."

Faye nodded. "Thank you."

All the way home in the police car, Faye wondered who would have wanted to kill Hank. She couldn't think of a single person.

When she arrived home, it was in the early hours of the morning and all she wanted to do was have a warm shower and wash all the wickedness and murkiness away. It felt like she was living a bad dream. She didn't want to be alone, yet neither did she want anyone near her.

The hot water jets pounded over her body and she untied her hair and let it fall down around her. Since her hair had never been cut, it reached way past her thighs, all the way to her knees. Normally she didn't wash it at night because of the length of time it took to dry. Right now, she didn't care if she caught a chill from damp hair.

For the next few hours she tossed and turned, and when it was light, she heard someone knocking on the door. She hoped it wasn't the police coming to arrest her for her husband's murder.

"Coming!" she yelled out. She quickly changed into a clean dress, wound her still damp hair in a towel, and opened the door. She was relieved to see Rain, her good friend, standing there.

"Oh Faye! I heard what happened from Bishop Luke."

Faye took hold of Rain's hand and pulled her inside the house. "I'm so glad to see you. It was dreadful." She told Rain everything that had happened.

Rain gasped. "And they think you did it?"

"*Jah!* I think so. I couldn't tell them a name of someone who might have wanted him dead, and they wanted me to tell them. There's no one. They asked me if Hank abused me. They think I did it in self-defense. They kept asking if I needed a lawyer."

"You look dreadful."

"I haven't had any sleep."

"Go upstairs now and get some sleep. I'll keep everyone away from you until you wake up."

"It's no use. If you've heard, everybody will hear and they'll be stopping by to see how I am."

"I'll keep them away. I'll tell them to call back another day."

"Would you?"

Rain nodded. *"Jah."*

"Denke. I haven't even told my parents or Hank's parents."

"The bishop said he'd do that. What you need now is some sleep."

"I'll try, but I don't know if I'll be able."

"Did they have a doctor look at you?" Rain asked.

"One of the paramedics examined me and gave me a couple of pills to help me sleep if I needed them."

"Did you take them?"

"Nee."

"You should take them, because if you don't sleep you might get into a bad pattern of not sleeping. Believe me, there's nothing worse."

"I can think of a few things. Like finding your husband dead, covered in blood in a buggy."

"I know. It must've been awful."

Tears fell down Faye's face once more.

"Try not to cry."

"I have to get it out. I can't bottle things up."

Rain nodded. "Cry after you've had a good sleep. Take the pills."

"I don't like taking things, and I don't know exactly what these pills are."

"It's not every day something like this happens, so I think you need a little bit of help to relax. Don't feel bad about it."

"I'll see how it goes. I don't know why I resist things like that. I might take them."

Rain smiled. "Now upstairs with you and get into bed. Would you like a cup of tea, or something?"

"Maybe a cup of hot tea will help me sleep. I don't know if I'll ever be able to sleep again."

Faye tossed and turned, and finally managed to get a little sleep. When she woke, the sun was high in the sky.

CHAPTER 3

*I*t was the morning of the day before the funeral and Rain came to the house. She told Faye it might help her feel better if they went out somewhere rather than Faye staying in the house all day.

The police were no further ahead with their investigations. All Faye was told was that her husband had been stabbed eight times, and so far they'd been unable to ascertain the location where the stabbing had taken place. All they knew from the blood evidence was that it had happened inside the buggy. The police had taken possession of the buggy as evidence, and Faye was glad she and Hank had a spare and three buggy horses. She was relieved that the horse Hank had been driving that awful evening was doing okay, having recovered from its fright once it had been returned to its stall after a soothing rubdown by Bishop Luke.

Just as Rain and Faye were about to walk into the markets, Rain stopped abruptly. *"Ach, nee!* I've left my money in the buggy. You wait here, I won't be a moment."

As Faye waited for Rain to return, she admired the flowers at the entrance. She was careful not to get too close. Where there were flowers there was pollen and where there was pollen there were bees. With her bee-sting allergy, she had to keep away from flowers as much as she could, but she loved to see all the beautiful colors. Faye jumped when someone touched her on the arm. She turned to see Hillary Bauer.

"Hillary?" she said in surprise. She hadn't seen Hillary for years. Faye knew that Hank had once dated Hillary, and then their relationship had ended abruptly. Hillary had been furious about it. She had left the community immediately and married an *Englischer.* Rumor had it that the marriage hadn't lasted long, and then she married another *Englisch* man.

"Yes, it's me," Hillary said with a quick laugh, and then her face turned serious. "I heard about

Hank, and I just wanted to say I'm very sorry for your loss."

"Thank you." Faye wasn't sure what to think about Hillary, with what she remembered from the past.

"It must've been horribly shocking to find him like you did."

"It was. It was a dreadful shock." Where was Rain? She looked over at the parked buggy and saw Rain inside moving about as though she couldn't find the bag that held her money. Rain had said she was going to protect her from everyone. Faye looked back at Hillary. "How did you hear about ...?"

"It was in the newspapers."

"Oh. I didn't know. I haven't left the house until now." Except for necessities, neither had she left the bedroom, or more accurately, the bed, but she didn't tell Hillary that.

"Do they know who did it?" Hillary asked.

"No, they don't. Are you living in these parts? I thought you moved away."

"I moved away when I married my first husband, and after he died I moved back here."

"Oh, your husband died?" Faye had heard she was twice divorced.

"Yes, my first husband died, and I remarried after

I moved back to this area. So, I know what it's like to lose a husband. Anyway, I just wanted to tell you that I'm sorry. Hank was a good man."

"*Jah*, he was."

"I must go."

She watched Hillary hurry away. The woman still had a mad gleam in her eye. A day after Hank had broken off their relationship, his barn had been set on fire, and he only just managed to get his horses out in time. Hank had always blamed Hillary for the fire and maybe he'd been right. Could Hillary have harbored anger for so long that it built up to the point where she wanted Hank dead? It didn't seem likely, since so much time had passed and the woman had married—twice.

"Sorry I was so long finding my bag," Rain said as she returned. "Who was that you were talking to?"

"That was Hillary Bauer."

Rain looked over at the figure in the distance. "I haven't seen her for years and years."

"She said her first husband died and now she's married again."

"I always wondered what happened to her."

Faye kept to herself that Hank had suspected Hillary of setting his barn on fire. "Let's get what we came here to get."

Rain stared at her. "Did she upset you?"

"*Nee,* I'm okay. She just brought back some memories."

"Of when she was in love with Hank?"

Faye nodded. "Something like that, *jah,* but that was a long time ago. Way before I married Hank."

"She always was a strange woman. Everyone wondered why he ended things with her so suddenly. I was only young back then, but my *mudder* liked to know everything that was happening and I found out too."

Faye walked into the farmers market wishing she'd stayed at home. Sooner or later, though, she'd have to go back out in public and today was as good a day as any. *Might as well get the first time over with,* she thought, *and then it'll be easier next time.*

"We'll hurry to get the food we need for tomorrow and then we'll leave," said Rain.

Faye nodded, glad that her friend was helping her with the food after the funeral the next day. Normally, the two of them made a day of it at the markets while Rain's children were at school. They'd linger, looking at all sorts of things, and then they'd stay for a cup of something and a bite to eat at their favorite café. But today wasn't normal.

CHAPTER 4

The next day at the viewing, Faye gazed at her late husband's lifeless body as he lay in the coffin in her living room. The funeral director had delivered his body to her house at daybreak. It was customary at an Amish funeral that the body be viewed at home before being driven to the graveyard in the specially designed buggy. Faye stared at her husband. He looked like he was asleep. The only difference was his face had taken on a paler gray tone.

There had never been any affection between them —well, not much. There had been respect, and no unkindness. It had been a marriage of convenience, in the sense that it was convenient for the rest of Faye's family and Hank, but inconvenient for her.

Faye stood back a little and greeted all the mourners as they poured in through her front door.

When Faye had a space between the visitors, Rain hurried toward her. "Hank's *bruder* is here."

"You mean half-*bruder*," Faye corrected her. Hank had two brothers, but they were both half-brothers to him, and oddly, to one another. Faye had always had a crush on John, one of Hank's half-brothers. He was closer to her in age than Hank, but he was still much older. She'd grown up hoping to marry him, but he left the community in his late teenage years. Her crush on John was something she had never shared with anyone, not even Rain.

"Half-*bruder*, full-*bruder*, what difference does it make?"

"It makes quite a difference to the *mudders*." Faye looked over the crowd. "Where is he?"

"Over near the door."

Faye wondered if Rain was talking about John, or the younger one, Silas. They stood on tiptoes and looked over the crowd, and then Faye saw him. It was John. She hadn't seen him for years. He looked a lot like Hank except he was better looking, and he didn't have Hank's grim, expressionless face. He was just as tall as Hank was with the same broad shoulders. John's coloring was dark and his face was pleasant with even features.

"John's a lot younger than Hank, isn't he?"

"*Jah*. When Hank's *mudder* died of pneumonia, his father married John's mother and then she tragically died in childbirth, and then later his father married Mary Anne, wife number three, and then they had Silas. That's why there's such an age gap between Hank and John and a smaller one between John and Silas." Of course, Rain knew all of this since Hank's family was in the same community and Hank's brothers had grown up with them, but it quieted Faye's nerves to talk.

Faye dug Rain in the ribs. "There's Silas now."

Silas had walked in behind John. Then came Silas' mother and then Faye's father-in-law. Mary Anne had raised Silas' older half-brothers as if they were her own. Hank stayed on in the community whereas John and Silas left the community as soon as they were old enough.

"When was the last time you saw John and Silas?" Rain asked.

"I haven't seen them since the wedding."

"Since your wedding?"

Faye nodded. "*Jah*. Hank didn't get along with them."

"Why not?"

"Who knows?" Faye shrugged her shoulders. "He didn't get along with anyone much."

Rain giggled. "You shouldn't say that, Faye."

"But it is the truth. He only got along with people he wanted to get along with. Only when it suited his purpose. And they'd both left the community."

"*Ach nee!*" Rain whispered. "Here comes your *mudder.* I'm going."

Faye's mother and Rain didn't get along, and Faye was certain that was because her mother didn't approve of anybody she liked.

Her mother arrived by her side, but not before frowning in disapproval at Rain's hasty getaway. "There's a big turnout today. Your husband was a very popular and influential man."

Faye turned around to look at the coffin. "And yet here he lies dead, and he had the same ending as everybody else. What became of all his hard work and the late nights when he missed dinner with me? None of that saved him from what happened."

Her mother opened her mouth in disgust. "That's a dreadful thing to say. He was a hard-worker and that's a good thing."

"*Nee,* it's not. He could've come home at a regular time and he never did. He hardly talked to me unless it was telling me what he needed me to do." She wanted her mother to hear loud and clear that she hadn't gotten over being forced into the marriage.

Her mother's lips pressed together.

Couldn't her mother just admit she'd made a mistake? Faye added, "I didn't ask much. I just wanted to be loved and looked after. He never told me he loved me and that's because he probably didn't."

Her mother leaned forward. "Don't let the police hear you say that."

"They can think what they want. I don't care. I just wanted a good marriage."

"And you had one. Not all men tell their wives they love them. What do words matter?"

"They matter to me."

"Well, did you bother to tell him that you loved him?"

She stared at her mother. She couldn't say right there at the funeral that she had never really loved him, but her mother should've known that. Why didn't she ever listen? It had never been a real marriage. The two of them had coexisted under the one roof, shared the same bed, and that was it. Instead of answering her mother's question, she referred back to her mother's previous comment. "Where did all the wealth and popularity get him?"

"I didn't say anything about wealth or money."

"He had a lot of money." And then it struck her fully that all of his money was now hers. As well as the business he'd built.

Her mother tipped back her head and spoke down her nose at her. "Speaking of wealth. I've arranged a family meeting for next week and we'll see which of your brothers is going to take over the company."

Faye narrowed her eyes. "What company?" Faye knew very well what company—her company, and her mother shouldn't have any say in the business she knew nothing about.

"Hank's company. It's now yours and one of your brothers will have to take over."

"*Nee,* they won't." Her mother had bullied her into the marriage and Faye wasn't going to let her bully her into giving up control of the company. Her company.

Her mother looked at her in surprise, her blue-green eyes bulging. "Are you going to employee someone to run the company?"

"You mean employ?"

Her mother frowned. "Don't take that tone with

me. I know nothing of business matters. You know what I meant. Someone has to run the company now that Hank has gone."

"I'll do it."

Her mother's mouth fell open in shock. "What do you know about running a company? You can barely run your household. If Hank didn't meet your expectations, I'm sure that likewise, you didn't meet his. *Gott* knows I tried to teach you all I knew, but you never listened properly."

She ignored her mother's mean comments. "I overheard a lot of Hank's conversations to his suppliers and such, and I'll be able to do it."

Her mother stepped closer and put a hand on her shoulder. "You're not thinking straight in this time of grief. You'll soon get that silly notion out of your head. Women just don't do things like that."

"Things like what?"

"Run businesses."

"Mother, that is nonsense. Abigail Gingerich has a very successful quilt store and employs six people."

"That's different. Hank employed nearly fifty."

"Forty-nine, and it's not different at all. Hank's business is larger, but it's the same principle."

"It's not the same, because Abigail's only got women working for her. You can't be in charge of men; it's absurd. A woman can't be in charge and above a man. You can't be a boss over your brothers. You're a woman."

Just when Faye was about to reply to her mother, they were interrupted by people who approached Faye to offer their condolences. Her mother stayed close by.

After the people moved on, Faye said to her mother, "Hank left the business to me. He left everything to me, and that means I have the say of what goes on in the business. And if any of the men aren't performing properly, I have a right to fire them, including my brothers."

Her mother gasped. "Don't you dare." She shook her finger at her, as though Faye were a misbehaving little child.

Embarrassed by her mother, Faye looked around, hoping no one was looking at them. When she didn't see anyone watching them, she turned back to her mother and desperately tried to get her point across. "This is my husband's funeral. Please don't speak to me in that way at this time. I'm a grieving widow."

Her mother lowered her voice. "You're probably happy he's gone. Now that he's gone, you're free to marry again. You never wanted to marry him in the first place."

"I won't lie. I didn't. You know you forced me into it. It was a huge mistake that I listened to you."

"I didn't force you into it. I just made you see common sense. With your *vadder's* failing health, he had to close his business. It was his dream that all his *kinner* work in the business that he built up, and you know that."

"Correction—you mean all of his sons, not all of his *kinner,* because I was never included."

"Women get married, they don't have to go out to work." Her mother held up a hand. "Don't tell me about all the women you know who have jobs. I don't want to hear it. Be at that family meeting on Tuesday night, and we together as a family will decide who's going to take over Hank's company. I think it should be Jacob since he's the oldest, but we'll just have to see. Maybe the task is too large for Jacob. Simon has more confidence and is better with people. Hank was good with people."

Faye scoffed.

Her mother gave her a steely gaze, daring her to utter a word. Out of respect for her late husband, Faye kept quiet. She had no intention of allowing any of her brothers to take over the company. None of them was cut out for it. She'd learn what to do and run the business herself.

SAMANTHA PRICE

As for ever marrying again, now that she'd already been married, she didn't know that she wanted any part of it. She was certainly not looking to marry again any time soon, as her mother had suggested.

As more people arrived, Faye's mother stood next to her greeting people as they came past the coffin. As much as she could, Faye put on a brave face. It wasn't easy being a widow at such a young age. It would've been easier if Hank had been sick and had slowly deteriorated. Then it wouldn't have been such a shock. The suddenness coupled with the fact that he'd been murdered was a double blow.

A little later, when Faye was by herself, Boris Lineberger walked over to her. He was one of the handful of *Englischers* at the funeral. He and Hank had worked together in the past and then he'd become a friendly business rival.

"I'm sorry about what happened to your husband."

She gave a little nod. "So am I."

He raised his eyebrows just slightly, seeming to be surprised by her response. It was hard to know what to say to people sometimes.

"I have some things I want to discuss with you, but right now is neither the time nor the place."

"What kind of things?"

"Business kind of things."

"Oh."

"I know where you live. I'll stop by your house to see you on Monday next week if that's all right."

"I won't be home. I'll be at work."

"Hank's work?"

"*Jah.*"

"Very well, that's where I'll find you."

She nodded. "Okay."

He tipped his head and walked away. She immediately knew that he wanted to take back some of the contracts that Hank had won from him. Maybe he figured the company might be dissolved with Hank's passing, and his firm would be able to benefit.

CHAPTER 5

When all the guests had gone home after the meal, Faye tried her best to relax. This had been a big day. First the mourners viewed the body at the house, followed by the trip to the cemetery, and then after the burial, people returned to the house for the meal.

At least she'd had a day free of police. From the day Hank had died until today, the day of the funeral, the police had been at the house every single day.

The day after Hank's death, Faye had allowed them to do a full search of the house and property. The police made her nervous, particularly Detective Hervey, who made her feel uncomfortable, almost guilty. She was certain he thought she'd done it and was looking for evidence so he could accuse her of murder. He even seemed annoyed that she'd admitted the knife they'd found was hers, but then she hadn't confessed.

After four nights without Hank, Faye was finally coming to terms with being on her own. Because Hank had worked such long hours, loneliness was a familiar friend. And with that absence of Hank from the home, she'd even become adept at doing odd jobs and maintenance work around the house, tasks that a man would've normally done. She sat down on the couch, glad that everybody had left and she was finally alone.

She'd never been in love, and she was sure most people had never been truly in love. In a general sense, she had an idea what love was, and before she married she used to long to be in love. That had made things worse when her mother told her she should marry Hank for the sake of her brothers. Faye had wanted to do the right thing to keep everybody happy. Hank had been a good provider, and apart from spending too little time with her, he hadn't been a bad husband. If he'd shown her the attention he should've, Faye might have been able to open her heart to him.

Faye kicked off her shoes and then swung her legs up onto the couch. When she was settled and comfortable, she ripped off her prayer *kapp* and tossed it onto the opposite couch. What was God's plan in taking Hank away so young? He was too young to die, and she was too young to be a widow.

THAT NIGHT, Faye was unable to sleep, but that didn't stop her from arriving early at work the next day. She had often helped her late husband with filing and general office work when the bookkeeper was on vacation. She overheard and discussed business with various people and figured she knew the workings of the company well enough to make a start of running it. The very thought of the meeting that night with her parents unsettled her, so she pushed it out of her mind the best she could.

After a briefing with Ronald, the office manager, Faye sat behind her husband's desk and leafed through the papers that he'd been going through on the last day he'd been there. She'd given instructions that no one touch anything in his office. Unfortunately, that didn't apply to the police. They had wanted to look through his office and Faye had given the okay. They informed her afterwards that they hadn't taken anything with them.

Spread over the top of his desk were orders that had to be processed and things that needed to be done, but there was nothing out of the ordinary. She was hoping to find a clue to who might have murdered him, but if the police hadn't found anything she didn't like her chances.

Two hours later, when she was deep in thought and up to her neck sorting out invoices and bills, she heard someone clear his throat. She looked up and in the office doorway was Hank's brother, John.

"John! I wasn't expecting to see you here today."

He slowly sauntered into her office. "We need to talk." He pulled out the chair and sat down opposite her. "I've come to offer you … relief."

"You're going to help me with this paperwork?" she joked, holding up a handful of papers.

"No. I've come to take this place off your hands."

She studied his face for a hint of a smile, then quickly realized he was serious. "What, the business?"

He smiled and nodded.

"That's simply out of the question."

The smile left his face. "I am Hank's brother and he would've wanted me to take over from him."

"You might've been his brother, but you barely

spent any time together these past years so I hardly believe you could know that."

"I grew up with him. I reckon I knew him better than anybody."

"I don't think so. You didn't visit once in all the time Hank and I were married."

He leaned forward. "That's only because I wasn't invited."

"Do you see my point? If you had been closer with Hank, or had stayed in the community, he would've invited you. Anyway, I'll be running the company from now on, since Hank left it to me."

John laughed. "Women don't know how to run companies."

"Many women run companies."

"Not of this size."

"Even larger than this."

"*Englischers* maybe, but not Amish women. It's not your place."

"It's the principle of the thing that matters, and it doesn't matter if the company is large or small. If Hank had wanted you to run it, he would've left it to you. I can run a company just as well as a man."

"What does your bishop say about that?"

"The bishop will be fine with it. As long as the company doesn't employ over one hundred people."

Faye vaguely remembered the bishop cautioning her husband that his business not get too big. If the business grew to the stage where it employed over one hundred people, he would've had to cut back somewhere, or maybe even divide the business somehow.

"Now that I'm here, you don't have to worry about any of that. I'll make sure you're looked after financially. With me running it, there's no limit to how big it'll grow. We can franchise it."

It wasn't herself she was worried about. She was worried about her duty to her brothers. Purely out of interest, she asked him, "What makes you more capable than one of my brothers?"

"From what I know of them, they're too young and have no experience. I've already franchised a coffee shop and sold it off. I'm looking to do something like that again." He looked around. "This business would be a perfect model."

"There's no use talking about it because it won't happen." Then a thought occurred to her. She should invite him to dinner that night to do battle with her mother. And then her mother might see sense in leaving her to run the company rather than Hank's brother. At the very worst, nothing would be resolved and no decisions would be made. "Actually, why don't you come to dinner at my *mudder's* place tonight?"

"That's very kind of you. I'm not sure that I should accept, though."

"Do you still live nearby?"

"Not far away. Nothing's that far when you have the advantage of owning a car. I didn't mean to sound ungracious just now. I'd be delighted to accept your offer as long as it's okay with your folks."

"*Jah*. You're Hank's *bruder*. It'll be fine." He looked so grateful to be invited that Faye almost felt bad for setting him up for an argument with her mother. Her mother was like an angry mother bear who would fiercely protect the business that kept her sons in employment.

"Faye, I'm not coming here to take away your company or take anything from you. I want to buy the company from you. I'm here to give, not take."

Faye shook her head. "*Denke,* I appreciate that, but it's not for sale."

"You haven't heard my offer."

She shook her head. "It won't matter."

"And what do your parents think about that?"

She had to tell him the truth even though her instinct was to keep him in the dark. "My parents want one of my brothers to be in charge."

He pressed his lips together, and his brow furrowed. "What does any of them know about management?"

"What do you know about it?"

He scoffed. "I've had vast experience. I just told you that."

"And nothing's going to stop you from doing the same thing as what you mentioned, but not with this company. Hank left it to me."

"Are you sure about that?"

"*Jah,* I'm sure." She noticed him smiling smugly. "What makes you ask that?"

"It seems odd that he would leave it to you."

"I was his wife."

"I'm just saying I think it's odd. Anyway, I'm prepared to buy you out, or come to some arrangement. Possibly a share of the profits when I grow the company. We could sell it off when it's built up and none of your family would have to work again—if all goes to plan."

"What would my brothers do if they didn't work? I've never heard of such a thing."

"I'll explain it all to them."

She sighed. "You can make a few suggestions tonight. You can be involved in a family discussion, since you're part of Hank's family—his earthly family at least."

"*Denke,* once again. I hope *they* can see sense."

She looked down at the papers on Hank's desk. It would take her hours to go through them. "I don't mean to be rude, but I've got a lot of work to get through. I'll see you tonight." Normally she wouldn't speak like that to anyone, but she considered that he had been impolite, the way he'd just barged in expecting to take over the company.

He leaned over and looked at the paperwork. "What are you doing? Maybe I can help you with it."

She snatched the paperwork away from him. "It's nothing I can't sort out for myself. Thanks all the same." She took a piece of paper from the side of her desk and grabbed a pen. "I'll write down my parents' address for you."

"Have they moved?"

"No."

"I remember where they live. I grew up in the community, remember?"

She nodded. "Vaguely."

"What time shall I be there?"

"Seven."

He stood up. "I hope your parents will see sense.

I'm a salesman, I'll bring them 'round to my way of thinking."

Faye hoped she was doing the right thing by inviting him. Either way, she had to do something with her time. Running the company was a challenge, and she liked the idea of seeing what she was capable of. However, it would be nice to have some support and if her family didn't support her, who would?

Faye called her parents' phone in their barn. After trying three times, her mother finally answered. She told her to expect one more for dinner that night. It gave Faye a small sense of satisfaction that having Hank's brother there would send her mother into a flap.

CHAPTER 6

*a*fter a day spent getting some of the paperwork sorted out, Faye left work and headed to her parents' house.

When she approached the house, she could tell by the absence of a car that their visitor hadn't arrived. Perhaps he'd thought better of doing battle with her mother. Faye giggled to herself. Yet, he wouldn't know what her mother was really like.

She secured her horse and walked into the house knowing all of her four brothers would have arrived home before her. Since none of her brothers were married, they all still lived at home.

Her mother pulled her aside as soon as she walked in the door. "Faye, what do you mean by inviting John Kirkdale? I was too shocked to ask this morning when you told me."

"He was interested to know what would become of the business, so I thought he should be here tonight."

Her mother frowned at her. "Why does he have any interest in it?"

"Because Hank was his *bruder* and besides that, he wants to take it over and do some franchising thing."

Her mother's face twisted into a scowl. "He what?"

"Wants to buy it, or run it—something like that. 'Sort something out,' I believe that's what he said. He might even think that Hank left it to him." Faye shrugged.

"Nee. Hank assured me he left it to you and your *kinner.* Since you never gave him any *kinner,* it's just yours now."

"We'll just have to see what John says tonight." Her mother had said that last part as though she believed Faye had deliberately withheld children from Hank.

"I still don't know why you invited him here. The boys would have an uncertain future if he took it over."

"Not if they do a good job."

"Faye! Are you saying you want him to take over?"

"Why don't we wait and hash this out when he gets here?"

Her mother shook her head. "Come and help me in the kitchen. I never could work out what went on in your head, and you haven't gotten any better as you've aged."

Faye followed her into the kitchen. "You make me sound like I'm ninety-five or something."

"I meant grown up. You know what I meant, but you'll never agree with me, will you?"

"I will when you're right."

Her mother shook her head again. "I just don't know who you took after. No one in the family is like you."

"Maybe I'm adopted."

"*Nee,* I can tell you that you definitely weren't. You caused me twenty-eight hours of excruciating pain when you were being born. You just didn't want to come out."

Faye had heard that many times. She was sure it was a gross exaggeration. "It can't have been that bad, *Mamm.*"

"You wait and see."

"I'll never know because I'll never be pregnant

because I'll never marry again." One thing she'd desperately wanted was a child. A child might finally have brought Hank and her together and they would've all been a family. Hank might've even come home from work earlier—early enough to have dinner with them.

Her mother turned to her with a wry smile turning the corners of her lips upward. "How do you know you're not pregnant already?"

Faye gulped. "I couldn't possibly be."

"Everything is possible. I had a dream you were pregnant."

"*Nee.* It's not possible."

"*Jah,* it is. Unless you and Hank didn't …"

"*Mamm!* I'll not discuss those things with you. Never say anything like that again to me, please." Faye covered her ears to drown out her mother's cackles.

When her mother finally stopped laughing, she said, "We're both women and it's only us in the kitchen. I'm sure you talk to your friends about things like that."

"I never do. That would be weird. Weirder still talking about things like that with you. Let's talk about something else, okay?"

"We can talk about why you invited Hank's half-

bruder to dinner. It's worse that he's an *Englischer* too."

"I already told you that, and anyway, he's family."

"You told me Hank hardly ever saw either *bruder,* and you said they never visited you even."

"He's still family, though. Once family always family, I guess."

"I suppose so. We can't make a habit of entertaining him, though." Her mother wrapped her hands in tea towels, leaned down, opened the oven, and pulled out the roast.

"That smells amazing, *Mamm.*"

She placed it on the wooden chopping block. "*Jah,* it does. You can't really go wrong with a roast. I suppose you found that out. Is that why you cooked Hank a lot of them?"

"They were his favorites."

"Hmm, I wonder why that was?"

Again, Faye ignored her mother's barbed comment. "What do you want me to do?"

"You can make the gravy using the pan juices. You always make it very well—without lumps. At least that's one thing I was able to teach you. It's a pity you can't have a meal out of gravy and nothing else. It's got so much flavor when it's made well."

"*Jah,* I do know how to make it without lumps."

Faye scooted her mother out of the way and took over the gravy making duties.

When they heard a car, her mother hurried out of the kitchen while Faye was stuck stirring the gravy over the stove. *I should've seen that coming,* Faye thought. Her mother had arranged for her to be busy so *Mamm* could talk to Hank's brother first. Her mother and father would be nice enough to John, but he certainly would not be leaving the house thinking he would be running the company, or that he would have a chance to buy it. Her mother was a very stubborn woman, and since his accident, *Dat* went along with everything his wife said.

Faye finished the gravy-making as quickly as she could, not caring whether the gravy had lumps in it or not. In her mind, it was more important to get out to the living room and hear what was being said. She placed the pan of gravy on a section of the stovetop where it would keep warm and then she hurried past the already set dinner table to see what was taking place.

When she saw John being greeted by her brothers, she leaned against the doorway of the kitchen and admired how handsome he was.

When he looked up and saw her, he flashed her a smile. "Hi, Faye."

"Hello, John. I'm glad you could make it."

"I told you I'd be here. And thanks again for the kind invitation."

"We're very happy to have you here," Mrs. King told him. She looked up at Faye. "Are we all good in the kitchen?"

"*Jah,* all done."

"Shall we eat?" Faye's mother said, looking first at John, and then everyone else.

"I'm ready," Faye's father said.

"Me too," one of her brothers said, and then all the men joined in, agreeing that they were ready to eat.

There was always plenty of food at Faye's parents' house. Her brothers had hearty appetites, and she figured that John would be just the same.

Halfway through dinner, Jacob, the eldest brother, asked, "When are we going to start talking about the business?"

John looked directly at Faye.

"*Jah,*" Faye's mother said. "John, you wouldn't believe it but Faye thinks she should run the company."

All of her brothers laughed, and Faye's father cast his gaze downward and shook his head as though he felt sorry for Faye for being so ridiculous. Faye kept quiet to hear what John would say.

John took a deep breath. "That's not right. A woman can't do something like that and be in charge of men."

"Quite right," her mother agreed.

"That's why I'm sure you'll see that I'm the best choice to take over the company. I've had three successful businesses of my own and I've franchised the last one and sold it for a small fortune. I'm even willing to take the company off your hands." The last part of what he said was directed to Faye's father, the head of the King household.

Faye could keep quiet no longer. "I don't know what you're looking at my *vadder* for, John. I think everyone's forgetting that the company's mine, and not anybody else's. It's got nothing to do with anyone else."

Silence swept over the table, and everybody looked at Faye. She didn't usually talk out like that, but she'd had enough. "I'm going to run this company, and nothing anyone will say or do can stop me. I was often with Hank when he was making important business decisions, and I got a pretty good idea of the direction to take the company."

John burst out laughing as if she had told a joke. "Direction?"

"Faye, don't you think you should give this some thought?" Jacob asked.

"I have thought about it. I've thought about what a good job I'd do in running the company. We, I mean I, employ a lot of people and that's a lot of responsibility, and I'm not taking that responsibility lightly. I know it's something I can do and I'll do it to the best of my ability."

"I think Faye would be good at it," Timothy, the youngest son, said.

"You're no expert," one of his older brothers told him.

"I'm entitled to my own opinion," Timothy said.

Their mother frowned at Timothy. "*Jah,* you can have your opinion, Timothy, but since you are too young to have any experience in these matters, perhaps you should keep your opinion to yourself and not try to enter into adult conversations."

"I am an adult, *Mamm*."

"Just finish off your carrots."

Now she was trying to embarrass Timothy into silence.

"I don't like carrots."

"Carrots are good for you. Just eat them and do so with a closed mouth."

John turned to Faye, saying, "I'm sure there are other things you can do with your time, Faye, like find a hobby. I'm sure there are many groups in the community you can join. Aren't there sewing or knitting circles? Aren't there things like that in the community?"

"*Jah,* similar groups. I can still do things like that if I choose to."

"Women just aren't cut out for business," John said, sounding a little frustrated.

"That's just ridiculous!" Faye knew she had to sound firm.

"Faye!" her father said.

Faye didn't like upsetting her father. She was used to upsetting her mother because her mother was constantly confrontational. Her father, on the other hand, was normally quiet and very mild tempered. "I'm sorry, *Dat.*"

"John is right."

John smiled when he saw he had Mr. King on his side. "How about this—I run the company for six months, and then we take it from there?"

Faye's parents looked at one another as though they were considering John's idea.

Faye knew she was outnumbered. Since she'd inherited the company, nothing would happen without her final decision, but she still wanted her family to feel involved. "Why don't I give that some thought?"

"That's the girl," her father said.

Her mother seemed pleased with the way things were turning out. "I'm glad you're starting to see sense."

"I thought you wanted me to run the company, *Mamm*," Jacob said.

"Maybe when you're older."

"But that's not what you said before Faye and John got here," Jacob persisted.

Her mother set her eyes on Faye, and said, "It's important that the company does well, and John has a lot of experience."

"I do, Faye," John said, staring her down.

When she had invited John, she never thought for a moment she'd be so ganged up on. Her idea had been they'd fight amongst each other. Timothy was the only one who believed in her. "As I said, I'll think about it."

Her mother leaned over and patted her hand. "I know you'll make the right decision."

"Pray about it," her father said.

"I will. I definitely will."

"Isn't anyone concerned about who killed Hank?" Timothy asked. "Aren't we overlooking that?"

Everyone remained silent. It was too painful for Faye to comment on. She still hadn't gotten over seeing him slumped in the buggy the way he had been.

Eventually, her father said, "*Gott* will judge whoever killed him."

"What if …"

"Enough said, Timothy." *Mamm* scowled at him.

When dinner was over and the men moved to the living room, Faye helped clear the dishes from the table. As she was placing a pile of dishes into the sink, she felt herself fading and lowered herself to the floor.

"What's wrong, Faye?" she heard her mother say as if from a distance but she couldn't even answer.

When the feeling passed, she looked up at her mother.

"You're as white as a sheet. What's wrong with you?"

"There's nothing wrong. My husband has just died, that's why I'm like this."

"I'm going to take you to the doctor tomorrow."

"There's no need for that. I'm okay. The para-

64

medics checked me out the other night, the night Hank died."

"I'm going to take you to the doctor, and that's that. You're not yourself. Take my hand." Her mother helped Faye to her feet. "Sit down at the table. Now about the doctor …"

"If that will keep you happy, I'll go tomorrow."

"*Nee*, that won't keep me happy because I don't think you'll go unless I take you. I'm going to call and make an appointment and I'll drive you there myself just to make sure you go."

Faye nodded. "All right. But I'll call and make an appointment to go there after work tomorrow."

"*Nee*, I'll call and make the appointment. On second thought, you can stop by and collect me and I'll go with you."

Since her mother was using her 'no-nonsense' tone, Faye didn't even bother arguing. "Okay, *Mamm*. You make the appointment, then call the office and tell me what time you've made it. I'll stop by and collect you."

"That's the girl."

Faye sighed. "But don't make it too early or I won't go. I've got so much to do. I'm sure I'll be fine. I just need a good sleep. A good nine hours would make me feel normal again."

Her mother nodded. "We'll soon see."

"Don't mention that I'm going to the doctor to John or *Dat* or anyone. I don't want anyone to worry."

"I have to tell your *vadder.*"

"Okay, but no one else."

Her mother nodded. "I'll take *kaffe* out to them and I won't mention a thing."

"And please don't talk any more about the business while John's here. Enough's been said."

"All right. I can see it upsets you. You sit there and don't move."

"I can't sit here when John's out there. It'd be rude."

"I'll get one of your *bruders* to take you home."

"*Mamm,* I'm okay," she said firmly. "I'll sit here for a minute and then I'll join them in the living room."

"You don't have to bite my head off." Her mother picked up the teakettle and filled it with water.

Somehow her mother always got the last word.

ON THE WAY home in the darkness, Faye was more than a little nervous, hoping she wouldn't meet the same fate as her husband. From what the detective had said, Hank was murdered by somebody who wanted him dead; the killer knew him. It wasn't some random killing. She didn't know if that was better or worse.

All Faye could think of was Timothy's question over dinner. Who killed her husband?

CHAPTER 7

The next morning at work, she looked up from behind her desk to see Mr. Lineberger walking into her office.

"Oh, this is a surprise."

"I mentioned at the funeral I'd stop by and see you."

"*Jah,* you did. Please take a seat." When he'd sat down in front of her, she swallowed hard. "What can I help you with?" She hardly needed to ask; she had a pretty good idea what his visit was about. Another person was going to try to take the company away from her.

"I'm here to help you with something. I'm here to make you an offer for the company. I assume it's now yours?"

SAMANTHA PRICE

"That's right, it is." At least there was someone who didn't have a hard time accepting that.

"Well, then I'm here to make you an offer."

"Thank you very much, but it's not for sale."

"I know you've got family working here. I'll keep all the same employees if that's what you're worried about. Well, I'll try to keep them employed as far as I can, but with merging my business with Hank's there's bound to be some layoffs."

"How can I be any clearer? Nothing is for sale."

He reached into his pocket and pulled out a business card. "My number's here in case you change your mind. It's a good idea that you sell, for everybody's sake."

She looked at the dark blue card with its white writing, and then looked up at him. "What do you mean?"

"Let's just say that selling to me might just be the safest for all concerned." His words had taken on a sinister tone.

"'Safest'?"

He nodded.

"I'm not sure I understand what you're saying."

"Hank ran this business and he ran it well. If someone's in charge who doesn't know what they're doing then things can head south pretty quickly. For instance, what do you know about health and safety requirements?"

She knew he meant for the factory where the workers used cutting and grinding equipment. "Nothing, but I'm sure there are rules and guidelines I can study up on. I'm used to working by the rules."

He shook his head. "It's not like baking a cake."

She rolled her eyes and didn't care that he saw her doing so. He was just the same as everyone else. All she wanted to do was be a success and run the company well. That'd show all of them.

He bounded to his feet. "I'll be in touch. Don't hesitate to call me if you change your mind."

"I won't." She stayed seated while he walked out of her office. When he was out of sight, she stood and hurried to the door of her office to make sure he walked directly out of her building, and to her relief he did so. She didn't want any competitors snooping about.

When she sat back down, she couldn't stop her mind from racing, trying to figure out who had killed Hank. Was it John, since he was so keen all of a sudden to step into his estranged brother's shoes? Or was it the jilted woman who'd wanted to marry Hank all those years ago? Or maybe it was Boris Lineberger since he was in direct opposition to

Hank. Hank had mentioned Lineberger's name to her and she knew he was in competition with Hank, and Hank consistently won contracts over him. With Hank out of the way, maybe Lineberger figured he'd be able to build his company further.

She jumped when the phone rang. It was her mother telling her what time she'd made the doctor's appointment.

AFTER FAYE HAD EXPLAINED to her doctor what had happened and described her fainting spells, he suggested taking blood and urine samples, which they did onsite. Once she'd done that, they had her wait back in the waiting room with her mother. Twenty minutes later, she was called back into the doctor's office and she sat down in front of him.

"Mrs. Kirkdale, I'm delighted to tell you that you're pregnant."

She sat there as the words sank in. How could she be pregnant when Hank was dead?

Yes, it was possible, but in all four years of their marriage she'd never gotten pregnant and this was the worst timing ever. She'd wanted a child while Hank was alive. There was so much she wanted to do now, and how could she do that and raise a child at the same time? "Are you sure you didn't get my sample mixed up with someone else's?"

He smiled at her. "I'm quite sure. I know this is probably a mixed blessing to you after your husband's just passed."

"That explains why I've been feeling faint."

"That will most likely pass as your pregnancy progresses. I'll recommend you an iron tonic."

"Iron?"

"It'll take a few days for the other tests to come back, but I'm certain they'll confirm you're low in iron which explains the dizzy spells. You have to build yourself up and eat properly for the baby's sake."

Baby? She was going to have a real live baby. "It doesn't seem real."

"It *is* real."

Her thoughts turned to her mother in the next room. She could not let her know. If her mother knew she was pregnant, she would be even more overbearing, and she'd insist on someone else taking over the company immediately. If John found out, he would be just as forceful in trying to take it over. "Thank you, Dr. Long. Now I know what's wrong with me."

He smiled at her. "Pregnancy isn't an illness."

"No, it's not. I would like to keep it secret for a bit, though. Thank you." She stood up.

"I haven't finished yet." When she sat back down, he said, "I wouldn't be doing my job if I don't ask you if you've got an OBGYN."

"Everyone in the community uses the same two midwives."

"Home birth?"

"Yes. We have our babies at home. Not all of us, but most of us. Is there anything else wrong with me or am I just low in iron?"

"The tests will be back in a few days. If everything's okay, we should be able to let you know over the phone. Or, you might have to be called back in. We'll see. Call us in three days."

"I'll call first, then, before I make another appointment."

"Very good." He ripped off a piece of paper and handed it to her. "That's the tonic I suggest you take."

She took it from him and folded it in two. "Thank you; I'll get it."

"I hope you rethink having a home birth."

"Women have been giving birth that way for thousands of years. It's normal. As you just said, pregnancy is not an illness."

"Giving birth can bring with it complications. I'd like you to have an ultrasound at the very least. They're routinely done at around six to eight weeks of pregnancy."

"I don't know … how far along I am."

He took some time to work things out with her. Then he filled out a form. "Take this to the hospital. I've written the address on the top of the form. Call them first and make an appointment for two weeks' time."

"Okay. I might do that."

"Please do. It'll give you peace of mind. You and me both."

"Thank you, doctor." She walked out of his office. After she had paid the receptionist, she turned around to face her mother.

"All okay?" her mother asked, searching her face.

She nodded and together they walked out into the street. "I just have to get an iron tonic. That's why I've been dizzy."

"That explains why you're so pale, too."

"I'll get it tomorrow."

"*Nee*. We'll go to the pharmacy right now."

There was no use arguing with her mother. After their visit to the nearest pharmacy, Faye took her mother home. Needing to tell someone her news, she went straight to Rain's house.

Rain would be the only person she would trust with the news. When she arrived, Rain was in the middle of cooking dinner for her family—her husband and their five children. The oldest two girls were helping in the kitchen, so Faye had to whisper.

"I've got surprising news."

"What?"

"I've just come back from the doctor and I'm pregnant."

Her friend's eyes bugged out. "Faye, that's wonderful news!"

"Is it? I'm not so sure."

"This is what you've wanted for years."

"It's just that it's come at the very worst time. How am I going to raise a child by myself? I could, but I don't see how I can do that and run Hank's company successfully."

"You won't be by yourself. You'll have the whole community there to help you, and you'll have me."

Faye smiled and nodded. "*Denke,* I can always rely on you with everything."

"I'm so excited."

Faye smiled at her best friend's excitement and wished that she felt half the joy that her friend felt.

"I'm not telling anyone just yet. You're the only one. It's like I had my life sorted out and I was going in one direction and just when I got comfortable, things changed, and then I changed my plans and after I just changed my plans, they changed again."

"Maybe you should just plan things less. One thing you know for certain is that the *boppli* will be coming in—how many months?" She looked over at her daughters. "Set the table now please, girls."

"The end of February. That's when the doctor worked out my baby will be born. It'll be cold," Faye said.

"Not too cold."

"It would be easier to have the baby in summer."

"It doesn't matter. Babies are born at all times of the year. Stop worrying about everything."

"It's become a habit, I'm afraid. And we still don't know who killed Hank and that's on my mind every day. I'm worried the police will arrest me. You know they think I did it?"

"Of course they don't."

"I think they do. They asked me why I changed my clothes and they put my clothes into a plastic bag and when I asked where my clothes were, they said they were 'in evidence.' Can you believe it? Evidence!"

"That's probably just the routine they have to do. Eliminate suspects, so they can find the real person who killed him."

"In my head, I know it's good about the *boppli,* but in my heart, I can't be happy until everything's resolved. I need to find out who killed him. The police said it must have been someone he knew." She bit her lip. "I can't have this hanging over my head. I'm scared all the time that I'm going to be next. Now I have to take care of my *boppli* and I don't want anything else bad to happen."

"We're finished, *Mamm,*" Rain's oldest daughter said.

"Okay, *denke*. Go and play and I'll call you when I'm ready to serve the meal."

The two girls ran out of the kitchen.

"Let's sit for a moment," Rain said.

When they were both sitting at the table, Faye said, "I'm sorry for coming over right at dinner time, but I've got no one else I can talk to. I can't tell anyone what's going on."

"That's fine. We can eat a little later than normal. Anyway, Ben's not even home yet."

Faye nodded.

"Now back to what we were talking about before.

If it's someone Hank knew, it could be someone you know."

Faye bit her lip again. "I didn't think of that. Do you really think so?"

"I do. Perhaps I know him too."

"Will you help me? If we can put our heads together we could find out who killed him and then, once that's out of the way, I can feel safe again and enjoy my *boppli*."

"Okay, I'll help."

"*Denke*. I've thought about it a lot."

"Tell me. Do you have some ideas?"

"Do you remember Hillary—"

"*Jah*, I do," Rain interrupted. "She was furious that Hank ended their relationship. She was always strange. She was a lot younger than Hank, too."

"Everyone was younger than Hank. Anyway, you're right, she was upset when Hank ended the relationship, I remember that."

"Me too. Do you think she burned down his barn?"

Faye shrugged. "Hank was convinced it could've only been her. The fire investigator said it was deliberately lit. But then there's John to consider. Why would he turn up suddenly and want to take over the business? I thought that was weird."

"Hmm, that's two. Anyone else?"

"*Jah*, Lineberger."

"The *Englischer* who was at Hank's funeral?"

"*Jah*, him. He wants to take over. He wants to buy the company. And I said no, and he wasn't too happy about it."

"That's three suspects. You know, this might be dangerous, trying to find out who killed him."

"I didn't think of that. Don't help me. Forget I said anything."

"There's no harm in us just asking around and making a few inquiries, is there?" Rain asked.

"I guess not."

Rain smiled. "Then that's what we'll do."

"I don't want to put you in harm's way."

"If it gets dangerous, we'll stop."

Faye nodded. "That sounds good. I'm too tired to think tonight. Let's both think of a plan of what to do and meet again in a day or two."

"Okay."

CHAPTER 8

*A*fter another gruelling day of trying to learn where the business was at, Faye had just sat down to her dinner at home when she heard a car pull up in her driveway. Being hungry, she popped a large bite of chicken into her mouth and hurried over to look through the kitchen window. Detective Hervey was just getting out of the car, and another man was getting out of the passenger seat. By the look of the other man, he too was a detective.

She hoped they weren't there to arrest her. Maybe they thought she did it because of the bloody clothes that she'd taken off and left in the mudroom.

She opened the door when they knocked. "Hello, Mrs. Kirkdale, we're sorry for this late hour. We

SAMANTHA PRICE

called earlier, but you weren't here," Hervey said. "This is Detective Wilson."

She nodded hello. "I was at the office."

"And we didn't want to disturb you there," the detective added.

"Thank you; I appreciate that. Come in." She stepped aside to let them in. "Have a seat in the living room." When they'd sat down, she asked, "Have you found out who killed Hank?"

"No, but we've been looking into some things that have provided a few names. Does the name Hillary Bauer mean anything to you?"

"Yes, I know Hillary. Hillary and Hank were together for a short time."

"The reason we ask is that over a ten-year period, your husband filed a few complaints against her."

"Did he? He never told me that."

"One was to do with a barn fire."

"That's right. He told me he thought she might have done that when he ended their relationship. And after that she was following him everywhere and sending him threatening letters. He didn't say he'd made official complaints, though."

"Then there was another serious incident a couple of years after the barn fire."

"Really?"

"Someone had attempted to burn down his barn again; they had doused it with gasoline. He walked in and caught someone fleeing the scene before they could do the job properly. Your husband claimed he suspected it was Hillary again."

"I had no idea." She jumped up when she heard a buggy approaching the house. "There's a buggy. I have no idea who that could be at this hour."

The detectives rose to their feet. "There are some more questions we need to ask, but perhaps you could come into the station tomorrow?"

"I could do that. What time? Can I do that at around five, after I finish work?"

Detective Hervey said, "How about you come in before work?"

"The quicker we move on things, the better," said Wilson.

"Okay. I'll be there around eight. Will you be there that early?"

"Yes. That's not early for me. I work all hours on a murder case."

Faye was pleased he was working so hard. "Thank you."

He gave her a smile, and somehow that gave her hope. Faye opened the door for the detectives to leave. They walked down the porch steps and headed to their car. Mrs. King gave the detectives a nod as she rushed past to her daughter.

"*Mamm,* what are you doing here?"

"I've come to see how you are."

"I'm fine."

"Have you eaten?"

"I was just in the middle of eating when the detectives arrived."

Her mother elbowed her out of the way and pushed her way inside. When she got to the kitchen, she looked down at Faye's dinner of chicken and vegetables. "Is this all you're having?"

"I already had some of it before the detectives got here."

"That's not enough."

"It's enough for me. Who's cooking for the boys?"

"They're looking after themselves tonight. I'm here to help you."

While Faye's mother fussed around in the kitchen, Faye sat down and finished her meal, all the while wondering if the police thought Hillary had some involvement in her husband's murder. They had to have, otherwise, why would they ask about her?

When Faye had finished eating, her mother

pushed her out of the kitchen and into the living room, saying she'd make her a cup of tea.

How could she get rid of her mother? Then she heard an excited-sounding scream coming from the kitchen. *What in the world?* she thought as she jumped up and ran in to see her mother holding up one of the baby jackets out of her secret stash of baby clothes she'd knitted over the years.

"You're pregnant and you didn't tell me?"

She plucked the pale-yellow jacket out of her mother's fingers. "These are clothes that I knitted just to keep myself busy." She didn't want to tell her they had been knitted in the desperate hope of becoming pregnant.

"You are pregnant and you found out at the doctor's. You were quiet all the way home. Plus, I had that dream."

Faye opened her mouth to speak, but the words wouldn't come out. Her mother had to find out sooner or later. Finally, she said, "Okay, *jah,* it's true, but I don't want anybody else to know just yet. It's too soon and I don't want a fuss made."

"When did you find out?"

"You were right. At the doctor's."

Her mother screamed again and pulled her into

her arms for a bear hug. "Oh, I'm so excited! The first of my *grosskinner!*"

Faye gasped for air. "Enough, *Mamm,* I can't breathe." After a few breaths, she said, "Remember, I don't want anybody else to know yet—no one, *Mamm.*"

When her mother finally left a few hours later, Faye wondered how many people her mother would tell. *Mamm* was never good at keeping secrets. It would only be a matter of time now before everybody in the community found out.

AFTER A FAIR NIGHT'S SLEEP, Faye went to the police station to see Detective Hervey.

"Thank you for coming in."

"Well, you asked me. Or rather, you told me to come. I didn't think I had a choice."

He looked at her strangely and she knew she'd been too rude. "I'm sorry we didn't get to finish what we were saying last night. My mother never stops by so late at night."

"I need to confirm with you who the beneficiaries of your husband's will are."

"He left everything to me."

"Everything?"

Faye nodded.

"What we didn't get a chance to tell you last night was that Hillary Bauer wasn't the only person your husband had filed complaints about."

Faye looked at him in surprise. "I don't know what you mean."

"Are you familiar with a man with the last name of Lineberger?"

"Yes, I know him. Hank had known him for a long time. They used to work together and they were friends."

"Yes, we're aware of a long association your husband had with Lineberger. Lineberger had been in and out of prison during the last few years on various charges. One time for forging checks and the other on embezzlement charges."

An image of Lineberger came into her head. He had certainly seemed like an honest man. "I had no idea. I just thought he was a businessman." He hadn't mentioned any violent charges, she noted.

"A very busy and industrious one it seems."

"He was at Hank's funeral, and he stopped in at the office and said he wanted to buy the company."

"I think what he's trying to do is get the company into his name somehow without paying for it. I wouldn't have any dealings with him if I were you."

"I won't. Thanks for warning me." It made her think about John's offer. She was sure John wouldn't try to swindle her and he'd be aware of sketchy business dealings and people who were out to defraud.

The detective leaned back in his chair. "Mrs. Kirkdale, you're a small fish swimming in a sea of sharks."

A shiver traveled up her spine. Although she had never been in love with Hank, she'd felt much safer when he'd been around. Learning that she was carrying a child and was now responsible for another life made her feel vulnerable. "That's kind of what I feel like. I feel like everyone's trying to keep me from taking charge of my company."

He suddenly lurched forward. "Someone else besides Lineberger?"

"Oh, it's nothing drastic. It's just that my mother wants my brothers to be involved with the business and she wants me to stay home and do nothing. She doesn't think a woman should run the company."

"Is there anyone else who's offered to buy you out?"

"Only Hank's brother."

"John Kirkdale?"

Her heart sank. She was just starting to trust John, and it scared her that the detective knew of him. Was he, too, a criminal? "Yes, John. Do you know him?"

"Only because we questioned Hank's entire family after Hank's murder."

Relief washed over her. "Of course."

"And what was your response when your brother-in-law asked to buy you out?"

"The same response as I gave to Lineberger—the company is not for sale."

WHEN MID-MORNING CAME, the last person Faye expected to see walking into her office was Rain.

"Hi! What are you doing here?"

Rain lingered by the door, and then she stepped into the office. "I thought about what we said about doing a little investigating."

Faye raised her eyebrows. "Sit down."

Rain sat opposite Faye with Hank's large desk in between them. "I figured we could start off with Hillary. So I found out where she works."

"Before you tell me that, I need to let you know I had a visit from the detective last night and right away he mentioned Hillary." Faye told her some of what the detective had said, and then asked, "Where does she work?"

"She works at a restaurant in town and I found out she starts her shift today at three. I thought we could accidentally bump into her at the parking lot before she gets to work."

"And do what?"

"I'm not sure. We could see what she has to say. See if she looks guilty."

"She didn't look guilty when I ran into her at the farmers market. But she still has that weird look to her eyes."

"We have to try something." Rain tapped her fingertips on the wooden desk. "Should we say something about Hank's barn fire, then?"

"*Nee.* I think that would be a bad idea. It was so long ago. *Denke* for finding out where she works, though. I should be able to slip away just before three today."

"*Gut.*"

"What about your *kinner* getting home from school?"

"The older ones can be in charge. I told them I might be late getting home."

Faye remembered looking after her four younger

brothers when they came home from school. Her mother was often out visiting or had long days at quilting bees and wasn't there when they arrived home. In larger families, the older siblings helped look after the younger; that was just the way it worked in an Amish family.

Rain said, "I'll get back here around two thirty then, and we can go together."

Faye nodded. "*Denke,* Rain. The police had more to say when they came to my *haus* last night. And this morning when I met with them at the station."

"What else did they say?"

"I forgot to tell you they asked me again if I could think of anybody else, besides Hillary, who might have killed Hank. I didn't want to name the people we discussed, but they knew about Lineberger and they had spoken with John already."

"Why didn't you want to name them?"

"Because not all of them are guilty. Maybe one of them is, and maybe not, but if the police ask them anything, they'll all suspect that I think they did it."

"I see what you mean. That would be awkward. Anyway, I'll see you back here this afternoon?"

"Jah."

.   .   .

LATER THAT DAY, Rain pulled up her buggy near the parking lot of the restaurant where Hillary worked, and both of them stepped out.

"What time is it now?" asked Rain as she secured the horse.

"It's a quarter before three."

"I wonder what time she arrives."

"How did you find out what time she starts today?"

"It wasn't easy. I found out from Elizabeth Yoder that she works here. Then I called the restaurant yesterday afternoon, pretended I was a customer who liked her service, and asked what time Hillary was working today."

"Ah, very clever."

"*Denke*. I thought so too. They had no problem telling me what time."

Faye shifted her weight from foot to foot. "What are we going to do? Are we going to just walk up and down the parking lot, or what? I don't want it to look like we're waiting for her."

"I found out from Elizabeth that Hillary drives a blue and white car, so as soon as we see that color car approaching the lot, we'll start walking up this way." Rain pointed up the street. "And then we'll act surprised to see her, and we'll call out."

Faye nodded. "Okay, but you'll have to take the lead in the conversation. I've got no idea what to say. And no running back to the buggy this time. I'm not comfortable doing this on my own."

"Okay. Leave it to me."

They were only at the lot for five minutes when an old blue and white car chugged into the parking lot.

"That must be her. Let's go." Rain pulled on Faye's sleeve and they started walking. Then they saw Hillary get out of the car and their eyes met hers.

Faye watched a man get out of the driver's seat after Hillary had gotten out of the passenger seat. The man was strangely familiar. She'd seen him before, but where? She couldn't remember.

Hillary waved, then said something to the man who walked away without looking up at them. Then Hillary called out, "Hello."

They walked over to her. "Hello, Hillary."

"What are you two doing around here?"

"We're just out doing a bit of shopping. What about you?"

"I work in that restaurant just there."

Faye turned to where Hillary pointed. "It looks nice."

"Actually, we've just finished shopping. We were shopping for tiny clothes because Faye's pregnant."

Faye couldn't hold in a large gasp. Rain knew not to tell anyone. Let alone the woman who had almost certainly burned down her baby's father's barn.

Hillary glared at Faye. "Is that true?"

"*Jah*, it is. Although, it's too early to tell people at the moment."

Rain's fingertips flew to her mouth. "Oh, sorry Faye. I forgot! I shouldn't have said anything."

"That's okay," Faye said, hoping her friend had just blurted out that information out of nervousness.

"Well, that is a surprise. You're not even showing at all."

"It's only in the early days."

"Yes, she's not due until February," Rain commented.

"And the baby is Hank's?" Hillary inquired through gritted teeth.

"Of course," Faye said. "I only found out just days after he left."

"You mean, after he died."

"He left to go home to be with *Gott*—that is what I meant."

Hillary continued to glare at Faye. "No matter

how the Amish sugar-coat death, dead is just plain old dead."

"Either way, he's not here," Faye said. Not wanting Hillary to be envious of her, she added, "I'll have to raise the baby alone."

"At least you've got something and you won't be alone. I'll have to go right now or I'll be late for work." She stomped away, and said over her shoulder, "Congratulations."

"Thank you," Faye called back. Then Faye looked at Rain and they both grimaced before they headed back to Rain's buggy. Hillary had been much nicer, Faye thought, when she'd bumped into her the day before the funeral. "Why did you have to tell her I'm pregnant?"

"It's the truth."

Faye stopped in her tracks. "Wait a minute. Did you plan this all along? Did you deliberately goad her by telling her I was pregnant with Hank's child to see what she'd say in anger?"

"*Nee,* of course not. I don't know why I said it. I'm sorry."

"That's okay. But we didn't really find out anything."

Rain started walking again and put her arm through Faye's. "We found out that she's still in love with Hank and always has been, and thus she's envious of you."

"But that doesn't mean she hated him and wanted to kill him."

"Maybe, and maybe not. They say there's a fine line between love and hate."

"I better get back to work. I can do another hour's worth before it's going-home time."

Rain drove Faye back to work.

wo nights later, Faye arrived home worried. How was she going to learn to run such a large business? Ronald, the office manager, was a good help, as were the other office staff, and none of them seemed put off by her being a woman, but she was worried Ronald would soon lose respect for her since she had come into this with no idea what she was doing. She was a fast learner, but there was a lot to learn.

With her baby coming, she didn't even know if she could keep up with the stress of working in Hank's business. Why was she struggling so hard? What would it matter if someone else took over the place? Maybe John was the best person to do that. She went into the kitchen to heat up some leftovers and suddenly she saw two bees at the window. Not believing her eyes, she took a closer look to see if they weren't large flies. No. They were definitely bees!

When one took flight, and flew directly for her, she screamed and ran out of the room. She knew she could die if she got stung, so she ran upstairs and shut herself in her bedroom. And then realized she'd left her EpiPen downstairs. It was times like these it would've come in handy to have a man in the house, or a cell phone. A man could get rid of the bees. It wasn't easy being single. Reminding herself she'd be both mother and father for her baby, she knew she'd have to practice being brave and doing everything herself. She'd been given a fanny pack to keep the EpiPen in and had done that for a while. Now she knew she'd have to wear it all the time. And she'd talk to her bishop about getting a cell phone, so she could call 911 if anything happened. Every second counted.

She opened a closet and pulled on one of Hank's suit coats. It covered her entire upper body once she turned the collar up, and the sleeves hung low and covered her hands. Seeing a towel over the chair, she grabbed it and covered half her face with it so only her eyes were peeping out. And then she pulled on a pair of Hank's trousers. They were far too big, so she tied them at the waist with her dressing gown cord, and then rolled up the legs so she could walk.

The bees couldn't sting her with all her body covered. With nearly every inch of her body covered in fabric, she trudged downstairs, summoning courage to get the bees out of the house. When she walked into the kitchen, a shiver traveled up her spine when she saw they'd left the window.

An idea occurred to her. If bees were the same as flies and mosquitoes, they'd travel to the light. She lit a lantern, opened the front door, and placed the lantern on the porch. Back in the kitchen, she took out a large flat kitchen spatula to swat them if they came near her. Then she saw they were back by the window. With a firm hold of the spatula, she pushed at them with the end of it to encourage them outside. One of them darted at her again, and she screamed and ran outside. As she ran down the porch steps covered in Hank's large suit and with the towel around her head, she was relieved to see a car.

Then she worried that the person in the car was Hank's murderer. Which was worse, facing the murderer or facing the chance of being stung by the bees?

She was relieved to see John jump out of the car.

He took one look at her and burst out laughing. "What on earth have you got on?"

Pointing the spatula toward the house, she said, "Bees."

He took a step forward, frowning. "What?"

She yanked the towel down to uncover her mouth. "Bees in the *haus*."

Then his face straightened and his eyes went wide. "Stay back." He headed into the house.

Everyone in the community had heard about her near death from a bee sting. The bishop had announced to everyone the importance of her staying away from bees, and if she was stung she was to be rushed to the nearest hospital. She was relieved that John remembered.

He came out a moment later. "Where did you see them? And how many?"

"In the kitchen. There were two." As he headed back in, she yelled after him, "Near the window."

He was gone for a couple of minutes and then he came back outside. "I opened the window and they flew out."

"The both of them?"

"Yes."

She sighed with relief. "Thank you, thank you so much."

"You're allergic, aren't you?"

"Yes, I am." Tears rolled down her face. Everything was overwhelming. She was suddenly alone in the world, trying to run a business she knew nothing about, and now the surprise pregnancy. How was she expected to do it all? She dropped the spatula she'd been clutching and covered her face with her hands. She didn't want to cry in front of her brother-in-law, but she couldn't help it.

He stepped closer. "It's okay, they're gone. Come inside." He put his arm around her shoulder and walked her inside. When he'd sat her on the couch, he asked, "Have you had something to eat?"

She shook her head. "I was going to heat up some leftovers."

"Sit down, I'll do that for you. Are they in the fridge?"

She nodded. "I've got no idea how the bees got into the *haus*. It's been closed up all day."

"Shall I go around and check all your doors and windows?"

"Yes please." While the food was heating, he checked the doors and windows.

She suddenly grew nervous. What if he was the killer and he'd come back to kill her? But why would he get rid of the bees if he was trying to kill her?

Faye closed her eyes and prayed. If it was God's will that she go to meet Him now, that she go home, then so be it. Right at that moment, she didn't care what happened to her, but now she had her unborn baby to care for. She put her life and the life of her baby in God's hands.

He walked back into the kitchen. "There's nothing open. But we need to see about getting screens on all of your windows, and probably on your doors. The bees must've come in when you opened the door this morning."

"But there's nothing with flowers around the house, I make sure of that. There's nothing to attract them. There aren't even any weeds. Hank and I kept all the weeds and everything down because of the allergy."

"How did you first know that you're allergic?"

"It wasn't my first bee sting. I'd been stung by bees before and it hurt but that was it. It was the third time, and I broke out into hives and then started to have trouble breathing. There was a doctor in the park who recognized the reaction. He and his wife rushed me to the hospital, and Jacob had to run home and tell my parents I'd been taken to the hospital."

"What happened at the hospital?"

"They told me later my blood pressure was dropping, and my heart rate was spiking. They say you'll never have a bad reaction on the first bee sting. Something to do with the body creating antibodies, and my body has too many and overreacts to the bee venom. I have to carry an EpiPen with me everywhere I go. They told me my next bee sting could kill me."

"That's dreadful."

"How did you know I needed you just now?"

He chuckled. "I felt dreadful about how I pressured you earlier. I stopped by to tell you that I'm sorry. It wasn't my intention to upset you." He cleared his throat. "I also heard today that I'm going to be an uncle."

"How did you hear? I only told a couple of people and I asked them to keep silent."

He shook his head. "It seems everyone knows. And my parents will find out sooner or later."

She'd have to tell Hank's parents. She wasn't looking forward to that and for some reason it hadn't occurred to her to tell them until John had just mentioned it. Of course, they'd want to know because her child would be their grandchild. "I'll tell them soon. I guess I'd better do that right away if the word is out."

He nodded. "When I heard the news, it made me realize something."

"What's that?"

"I've been chasing money and that's not really important. What's important is family. I left the community at a young age wanting to make something of myself. I had a yearning, a deep yearning that I had to be successful. Today, I had an epiphany. You make something of yourself the moment you let go of needing to make something of yourself." He shook his head. "Everything that I thought was important isn't."

"And how did you realize this?"

"When I heard the news that my brother—my late brother—was having a child. I realized that's what I want. I'm going to change my life and come back to the community."

It pleased Faye to hear the news. "That's a big decision."

"Well, I need to make big changes. I've never been scared of facing challenges. I made myself a new life once before, and I can do it again."

She realized that she was hoping he was going to propose to her. She had always been able to sense something between them. Perhaps she would've married him if her mother hadn't forced her to marry his older brother. Maybe the next thing was he'd ask her to marry him. Her baby would have a father, and how perfect would that be that her baby's stepfather would also be his or her uncle? There would be such a bond.

"And you know what else, Faye?"

"What?" Her heart thumped in anticipation of a proposal. Of course, he'd have to take the instructions and be baptized before they married.

"I think I've burned your food." He jumped up and raced to turn off the oven.

She sniffed the air. And then she laughed at herself for getting carried away. "I think you have, but we can't open the windows or those bees will fly back in."

"I won't open the oven door either, or smoke will fill the room. I'll take you out for pizza."

She looked down at herself in Hank's old clothes and with the towel still draped about her neck. "Looking like this?"

He chuckled. "Why don't I bring a couple of takeout pizzas back? It won't take long."

"Thank you, I'd like that."

"I'll be less than half an hour."

When he drove off, she headed to the shower. The least she could do was make herself look presentable for her dinner guest. She was pleased he was coming back to the community. Even though he hadn't asked her to marry him and probably had no intention of doing so, at least her child would have an uncle on his father's side who was in the community.

THE NEXT DAY was the day to call the doctor for her blood test results. When they wouldn't give her the results over the phone, Faye started to worry. What if she had something seriously wrong with her? She was far too young to die. There were things she wanted to do and experience in her life, and besides that, she didn't want to have an illness where she would linger and be a burden to others. She made an appointment for that very day.

Her mother had forgotten she had other tests results coming in. She'd been too busy being delighted about becoming a grandmother. Faye's baby would be her mother's first grandchild.

After waiting three quarters of an hour in the waiting room, the doctor gave her the all clear. Faye was more than relieved, and on the way home she stopped by Rain's house to tell her about the altercation with the bees.

. . .

"DON'T YOU SEE, FAYE?" Rain asked, as they sat drinking hot tea in the kitchen. "The bees were placed in your house by Hillary."

"How?"

"I don't know. She probably had one of those insect catchers that children have, or she could have caught them in a jar. Did you lock your door?"

"I lock it when I'm inside, but I don't always lock it when I'm out. Do you really think she did that?"

"*Jah,* she was angry that you're pregnant. That's what she wanted—to be married to Hank and have his *kinner.*"

Faye slowly nodded. "She killed Hank in a rage, and then she tried to kill me?"

Rain nodded.

"Why not stab me, too?"

"The police are already on her trail. That's what you said, and she wouldn't want to give them more reason to think she did it. You should tell the police about it."

"Do you think so?"

"I do. I'll come with you. You should go there now."

"It's late. The detective's probably not working at this time."

Rain bounded to her feet. "Let's call him from the barn."

Faye called the detective and made an appointment to see him that night, and then told Rain she'd go by herself.

With her pregnancy, Faye was growing increasingly tired. It was either from that, or from working every day trying to fill Hank's shoes. Or maybe a good bit of both.

SHE WAS SHOWN into the detective's office when she arrived at the station.

He looked up when she walked in. He stood up and reached out his hand. When she shook it, he said, "What can I do for you?"

"Firstly, are you any further ahead in your investigations?"

He shook his head. "I'm afraid not. Please take a seat."

She sat down. "When I got home yesterday afternoon, there were two bees in the house." After she took a deep breath to settle her nerves, she looked up at his blank face. "I'm deathly allergic to them and everyone who was in the community when I was around fifteen knows that I nearly died when I was stung by a bee. I came way too close, and the doctor said the next sting could kill me."

"I'm sorry, but I don't know where you're going with this."

"A friend of mine thought that someone might have done that deliberately."

"Put bees in your house to bite you?"

"Sting."

"What? Oh. Pardon me, to sting you?"

Faye nodded. "It might sound silly. I suppose it does, but I told my friend what happened and she was insistent that I tell you."

"Who knows about your allergy?"

"Everyone who was in the community when I was fifteen and was old enough at the time to remember it."

"That would include Hank's half-brothers?"

"Yes, it would, and it would include Hillary Bauer."

"I see where you're going with this. You think Hillary put bees in your house?"

"Possibly."

"Why would she wish you harm? Your husband's gone so it wouldn't be to get back at him."

Faye took a deep breath. "I just found out that I'm expecting and I don't think Hillary's happy about it."

"How did she find out?"

"My friend and I bumped into her and somehow my friend blurted it out."

He clicked on the end of his pen. "What's the name of this friend of yours?"

"Her name is Rain Hersler."

He jotted the name down and then looked up at her. "Tell me what happened yesterday from the time you arrived home."

She told him everything that had happened, including how John arrived unexpectedly and saved the day.

"He arrived just in time to eradicate the bees?"

"The bees weren't harmed. He opened the window and they flew out."

"Interesting." He jotted a few more things down. "You should really have window screens, with that allergy." Then he looked up at her and smiled. "Congratulations, by the way."

"Oh." She giggled. "Thank you. It was a surprise."

"Has John been stopping by regularly?"

"*Nee,* he never stops by, but I was sure pleased to see him."

"Hmm. And how long has Rain Hersler been your friend?"

"For as long as I can remember. Why?"

"I'm just getting a broad picture."

"Rain wouldn't have anything to do with Hank's murder."

He put his writing pad down and looked across at her. "Have you seen any more of Lineberger?"

"I haven't."

"What about John's brother?"

"Silas?" she said in a startled tone.

"Yes."

"No, I haven't seen him since the funeral. Do you suspect him?"

"We've had to talk with everyone who was close to Hank. Starting with close friends and family. Although, we haven't found it easy to get information from those in your Amish community."

"Oh, I'm sorry." He never answered her question directly and she wondered why. She made a mental note to tell Rain about that. "I'm not sure whether I should've told you about the bees or not. I don't want to waste your time."

"You're not wasting my time. We need to explore

all avenues; we never know which piece of information will turn out to be important."

"That's good. I'm glad."

AFTER A PARTICULARLY GRUELLING episode with Ronald, the office manager, Faye was nearly in tears. It was so hard juggling so many things, from the staff to overseeing orders and the quotes, plus a dozen other jobs. She closed her office door, picked up the phone, and called the phone in Rain's barn, hoping she'd be close by to answer it.

"Hello?"

"Rain!"

"Hi, Faye. Is everything okay?"

Faye sniffed back tears. She felt guilty for not being deliriously happy about the baby, and guilty for not having been in love with Hank. "I don't know if this is what I want anymore—to run this business."

"This is what you wanted before, so don't let a *boppli* change your plans."

"But it does."

"Don't make any decisions until you feel better. Why don't I move in with you for a couple of days?"

"*Denke,* but *nee,* it's okay. I'll get over it. I'm just so tired. How am I going to do everything?"

"You'll take the *boppli* to work with you, or you'll get a nanny to work a few hours a day."

"I don't know."

Rain gave an exasperated sigh. "Well, just give your business over to John to run, then."

"I might have to. I don't want to, although I don't see any other way around things right now."

"Something's got to give and you don't want it to be your health, or your *boppli's* health."

CHAPTER 10

When Faye got to work a gruelling week and a half later, she was expecting another typical day. Mid-morning was when she checked the calendar and realized what day it was. It was the day she was supposed to have her ultrasound. She'd been so busy trying to keep her head above water in the office, she'd forgotten completely.

She had to be there at eleven o'clock. She found Ronald and told him she would be going out for a while. There was just enough time to get there by taxi.

When she walked into the hospital, she had no idea where to go. As she was looking around, she saw Hillary and a man who was with her. The same man who had been with her in that blue and white car outside the restaurant. They got into an elevator and the door closed.

She hurried to the elevator and watched the red digital numbers. It stopped at floor two. She pressed the button and the elevator returned and the doors opened. They'd definitely gone to level two. She stepped into the lift and read the directory. Floor two was the oncology department. She was pretty sure that was for the cancer patients.

Did either the man or Hillary have cancer? Which one? She pressed the button to floor two after she got in the lift, and the doors closed. When the elevator doors opened, she was faced with a blank wall; she could either go left or right. She chose right and walked a little way, and then to her left was a large room. She saw that it was the chemotherapy treatment room. She had an uncle who'd had cancer and she had gone with him to some of his treatments to keep him company. She had a quick look into the room and then ducked back around when she saw a nurse setting Hillary up for treatment while the man leafed through a magazine. She ducked back so no one could see her.

"Can I help you there?" She turned around to see

a man wearing blue scrubs. He was either a nurse or some kind of orderly.

"Yes, I'm lost. I've come here to have an ultrasound."

"You'll need to go to the floor below, level one."

"Thank you." She smiled at the man and hurried back to the elevator.

SHE FOUND her way to the place she was supposed to be and minutes later cold gel was moved across her abdomen, and she was having an ultrasound performed.

"CAN you tell whether it's a boy or girl yet?"

"Not at this early stage. Maybe in the next ultrasound."

"I'll only be having this one ultrasound, if everything's okay. I don't think I'd want to know anyway."

"Your baby looks just fine, Mrs. Kirkdale. You'll get the official report from your doctor."

Faye was relieved and a tear trickled down her face. "Thank you."

Rather than heading back to work, she stopped at

Rain's house to tell her what she had seen on the second floor of the hospital.

"ARE YOU SURE?"

"I am. It was a chemo treatment room. I've been in one before. It was a different hospital but I know what they look like."

"So, Hillary has cancer?"

"Yes, and who was that man with her?"

"That's obviously her new husband."

"I guess that makes sense. I just wish I knew where I've seen him before. Can you go back to Elizabeth and find out everything you can about Hillary and her husband?"

"She's going to wonder why I'm asking her all these questions."

"I don't care. I don't care if it looks suspicious; make up a reason if you like. And remember to tell me every little thing she says."

"Okay, I'll go now before the children get home from school."

"Thanks."

When Faye arrived back at work, Silas was sitting in her office behind her desk going through paperwork.

"Silas."

He slowly looked up at her. "Faye, nice of you to show up for work."

She walked towards him. "I've been here every day. I had an urgent appointment to get to." Feeling she needed to explain her absence, she said, "For my baby."

"Yes, I heard about that. That's why I'm here. You're going to need help and I'm here to give it to you."

"Help?"

"I'll give you two choices. We go fifty-fifty. You give me fifty percent and I'll run the company and you'll get half the profits. Option two is that I'll buy you out."

"I told John and I'll tell you, the company is not for sale."

"I was hoping you would say that. I can always take it from you and then you won't get a cent."

She stood there staring at Silas, wondering whether he had killed his half-brother. Hank must have been killed for money, she figured, and specifically for his company. The murderer had to be someone who wanted it, and she was standing in the murderer's way.

All of Hank's family would've thought the business should go to one of Hank's brothers on his passing. But surely the killer would've found that out beforehand.

"You're in my seat," she said, standing her ground.

"Did you hear what I just said?"

"How do you think you're going to take the company from me?"

"Declare you incompetent. That'd be easy, and perhaps you are even insane if you think you can run a company like this with no experience. Anyway, you won't get a cent from my brother's estate when they prove that you killed him."

Her mouth fell open at his words. "How dare you say a thing like that to me? You probably did it, and you're upset that Hank didn't leave the company to you and John."

"If you cooperate with me, I'll help you with the police."

"I don't need help with the police and I don't need help with the business." That wasn't completely true; she probably needed help with both, but not from him.

Now Silas was on the top of her suspect list. She wondered what the police had found out about Silas. "Who let you in here?"

"I just walked in."

"Does Ronald know you're here?"

"I sent him off on an errand."

"What?"

He nodded.

"You've got no right to order my staff about."

"They need and want to follow a man, not a woman, and especially not an Amish woman."

"Leave now, or I'll call the police and have them drag you out."

He raised his arms. "I'm sorry, I think we got off on the wrong foot. Let's start again."

"Let's not. Get out!"

Without taking his eyes off her, he slowly rose to his feet. The cold, cruel look in his eyes turned her insides to stone. She did her best not to let it show how much he scared her.

"I'll give you a day or two to think things over and then you'll say what I say make sense. None of the staff wants you here," he continued. "Except your useless brothers."

By this time, he was halfway across her office floor. "Get out!" she yelled.

He slowly walked out the door without looking back. When she had watched him all the way out of the building, she sat down on the chair behind her desk, relieved that he was gone. And then his words came into her mind. What if it was true that none of the staff wanted her there? Who would want to follow a boss who didn't know what they were doing? The thought occurred to her that maybe John had sent Silas to be horrible and that way John's offer would seem that much more attractive. Were Hank's two half-brothers in this together?

She hoped that John was for her and not against her, as she was starting to develop feelings for him. But were they real feelings or were they feelings born out of her vulnerability, since she was suddenly alone and pregnant? Did she see John as an answer to her problems, a substitute for Hank?

All she knew was that she couldn't rest until she found out who had killed Hank. Until the police found out who did it, she would be unable to trust anybody. She felt like she was on a fast-moving conveyor belt taking her from one disaster to another. She closed her eyes and took a couple of deep breaths and then she picked up the phone and called Detective Hervey to report what had happened and to see if there had been any new developments.

CHAPTER 11

The detective was out, so she left a message for him to call back. Just as she was about to go through the next stack of paperwork, an image of Hillary's man came into her head. Aha! She remembered where she had seen him before. A couple of years ago, he had knocked on her door asking questions about Hank, saying he was looking for a man who was adopted into the Amish. She gave him the address of Hank's parents. A couple of days later she had a conversation with Hank's step-mother who hadn't been too pleased to get a visit from this man asking her questions surrounding Hank's background.

Was Hank adopted? And could his birth family have anything to do with his murder?

Just when she was leaving work for the day, she got a call from Rain. "Hello, Rain. Did you talk with Elizabeth?"

"I did, and I found out a lot. I described the man who was with Hillary, and Elizabeth said that that's her husband. And the restaurant where Hillary works—she owns it, that one and several other restaurants. She's a very wealthy woman. The husband who died owned a string of restaurants and she inherited them."

"Really? That is interesting. If they're rich, why were they driving that old beat up car?"

"Elizabeth said they collect rare vintage cars. That must've been one of them."

"Oh." Faye didn't know one old car from another and neither did Rain. "Anything else?"

"Isn't that enough?" Rain asked.

"*Jah,* it's quite a lot. *Denke* for finding that out. Does Elizabeth know that Hillary's sick?"

"She didn't mention it, so I didn't bring it up."

"That's best." Faye told her friend about Silas' visit and him turning nasty. Then she told Rain of her theory about Silas and John being in it together.

"Have you told the police any of this?" Rain asked.

"*Nee.* I called the detective earlier and left a

message for him to call me back. But I worry that it's just a whole jumble of things and nothing concrete. Silas and Hillary might have nothing to do with Hank's murder. What if the police were wrong and it was just a random killing?"

"I don't know, but that's for the police to figure out."

JUST WHEN FAYE had gotten into her house, John arrived and knocked on her door.

"John, come in."

Am I letting a killer into the house? She decided not to mention Silas' visit and see if John mentioned it.

"How have you been?"

"Fine."

"Have you eaten?"

"I'm just making myself some dinner. You can join me."

"No, I won't keep you long. I just wanted to tell you that I've spoken to the bishop. I'm tying up a few loose ends over the next few days and I'll be back into the community next week. I'm taking the instructions and being baptized. I'll be a fully-fledged member of the Amish community before you know it."

Now all suspicion of him went out the window. He was really doing this, not just talking about it. "Really?"

He nodded.

"That makes me so happy."

He chuckled. "Me too. It hasn't been an easy decision and I know there will be hardships along the way and big adjustments to make, but I know I'm doing this for the right reasons—"

"What reasons?"

She wondered if she was one of those reasons— that's what she hoped.

"I want to live the best I can, for myself, for others, and for God. I figure that is more reasonable service, since God gave me this life. There's so much suffering and so much pain everywhere I look. It'll be hard for me to give some things up, but I'll be gaining so much more. I want a family and I couldn't imagine having a family in the world and raising children in a society that's collapsing. I want to raise my children within the structure of the community."

She nodded.

He continued, "And to think your child will be my children's cousin. That's a good start."

She forced a smile, but inside she was crushed. He wasn't seeing her as a potential wife at all. At least now she knew for certain. "It looks like you'll have a busy few days ahead of you."

"You've got no idea. I hardly know where to start."

They stared into each other's eyes for a moment, before he said, "I'll let you get back to your dinner." He turned around and walked out the door.

She took a couple of steps and put a hand on the front door.

He turned around. "Please let me know if you want anything, or if I can do anything for you."

"*Denke*, I will."

She watched while he got in his car and drove away.

IT WAS at the Sunday meeting that Faye came face-to-face with Hank's stepmother. Faye took the opportunity to ask her about the visit from that man, Hillary's husband.

"Do you remember a few years ago a man came to your door asking about Hank and adoption?"

She raised her head. "I do. The man that you sent there. Did you think Hank was adopted, or something?"

"*Nee*, I never had cause to think that at all. The

man came asking me questions about Hank and whether he was adopted, and I said to my knowledge he wasn't. Then he asked for your address and I saw no harm in giving it to him."

"He wasn't adopted," she snapped.

"I didn't say he was, but do you remember anything about the man, anything at all?"

"No. Like what?"

Faye shook her head. "I don't know. I thought about it the other day, that's all. It was odd that someone would come around asking questions like that."

"I suppose he was just a man searching for his family."

"Did he say it was for his family?" Faye asked.

"From what I recall, he said he was searching for his wife's brother and that he'd been adopted into an Amish family."

"That's interesting."

If that man had been telling her the truth, that meant that Hillary had an adopted brother within the Amish. Did that mean Hillary was adopted as well? Who would she ask? Hillary's parents had long since died.

Faye rushed across the yard intending to report

her findings to Rain, but before she got there, John signalled to her.

Then he walked toward her.

"Hi, John. How did you enjoy your first meeting back?"

"*Wunderbaar.*" He chuckled.

"I'm glad."

"I'll have to get used to speaking Pennsylvania Dutch again."

"That won't be too hard since you were raised speaking it."

"I guess. Where are you hurrying off to?"

"Oh, just to talk to Rain."

"You and Rain were always so close."

"She's been my best friend as long as I can remember. I only have brothers, so she's like a sister to me."

"Really?"

She studied his face. The way he said it was as though it wasn't a good idea to be Rain's friend. "Why do you say it like that?"

"Oh, nothing."

"Do you know something I don't know?"

"About Rain?"

She nodded.

"I've just always thought it's best to have a lot of

friends rather than just one friend. If one friend disappoints you, it doesn't matter so much because you have so many others. But if you only have one friend and she disappoints you then you have no one." His eyes bored through hers as if he was giving her a hint about something and didn't want to say something negative about Rain.

Now she felt like she couldn't trust anybody. "Silas came to see me at the office the other day."

"Did he?"

"Did you know he was coming to see me?"

"I haven't talked to Silas since Hank's funeral."

"He wasn't very nice. He seemed to be threatening me or something."

John frowned. "What did he want?"

"He wanted me to give him half of the business, and he'd run it and he said we'd split the earnings."

A wave of fury covered John's face.

"Then he wanted ... I don't know. It's just everyone has so many demands on me lately I just don't know whether I'm coming or going." She rubbed her eyes, realizing she was close to tears.

He put a hand on her arm. "Sit down, Faye. You've had far too much pressure on you." He led her over to a chair. "Can I get you something to eat?"

She nodded and looked back at the large table of

food and all the people who were helping themselves. She had no energy to get any food for herself. "If you could just get me a little something I would appreciate it."

"Stay here, I'll be back."

She thought how good it would be to have him for a husband, so he could look after her.

On her way home, her horse pulled the buggy through the streets while Faye thought of the empty home that awaited her. Sunday was one day when Hank had been there.

There was never much traffic on a Sunday when she drove the buggy home from the meetings and Faye was surprised to hear cars zooming behind her. She glanced over her shoulder and saw two black cars. One overtook her and was so close that her horse jumped to one side, causing the buggy to lurch too. The next car accelerated and clipped the back of the buggy. That's when she knew these cars were only out to harass her. Then the car honked the horn and clipped the buggy again. She pulled the buggy over off the road and the car zoomed off. She tried to see who was driving but the windows were darkened.

Her horse's neck was held up and his ears were turned back. She waited a while until both she and her horse were calm. Making sure there were no cars around, she got down to inspect the buggy, the horse, and the harness. When she saw everything was okay, she patted the horse and spoke to him in soothing tones in an effort to calm him. The black cars had meant to frighten her and they'd done just that.

When she climbed back into the buggy, Lineberger came to mind. He'd threatened her. Maybe it was he who'd sent the people in that car to give her a warning.

As soon as Faye turned the horse out into the paddock, she picked up the phone in the barn to call the detective. What was he doing about finding Hank's killer? Not much, it seemed. She'd been living in fear since he'd been killed and she couldn't take it anymore. Each day she drove home half expecting that someone might jump into her buggy and stab her. Either that or in fear she'd arrive home to a house full of bees.

She called the detective's cell phone. When he answered, he sounded like he'd been having a nap.

"Hello, Detective, it's Faye Kirkdale."

"What can I do for you?"

"You can find my husband's killer," she snapped. "Now someone's trying to kill me. I was harassed by two black cars. One just missed me and the other hit me from behind deliberately—twice. I'm sure it was something to do with Lineberger, that man who's trying to buy me out. He said something about me being foolish and I might be in danger if I didn't take his offer."

"Are you injured?"

"No."

"Did you get the plate numbers?"

"I didn't even think of that." Faye felt stupid for not doing something so simple. "Anyway, what have you been doing about finding who murdered Hank?"

"We've been working on it and following up leads."

Faye gave an exasperated sigh. "It's not good enough. I live every day wondering if I'll be next. I'm having a baby soon and I'm worried about my child's safety. I want you to find the killer before I give birth."

"I had forgotten you were expecting."

"Well, I am."

"We're doing all we can. Do you have any new information?"

At the risk of sounding silly, she also told him

about Silas' visit to the office and about Hillary's illness and Hillary's husband's visit to her some time ago inquiring about whether Hank might have been adopted.

"Leave it with me," was all that he said.

"I've been leaving it with you for too long." She slammed the phone down, and then picked it up and called a taxi. She opened the phonebook and found the address of Hillary's restaurant, and then she found Hillary's home address. She'd try her home first and then confront her about this adoption business and find out what was really going on. Tomorrow, she'd work out what was going on with Silas.

She arrived at Hillary's house and knocked on her door. She listened to heavy footsteps as they approached the door.

"Oh. Hello. I hope I've got the right place. I'm looking for Hillary Bauer. I suppose she has a different last name now."

"That's my wife."

"Is she home?"

"She's at one of our restaurants."

Before she could stop herself, she said, "Isn't she sick?"

"Yes, but she won't stop working until she drops.

That's just who she is." He studied her. "Have we met before?"

"I don't know."

"Hillary knew you when she was Amish?"

"That's right."

"She should be home any minute. Come in and wait for her."

"Thanks." When he stepped back, Faye walked in.

He showed her to the living room and sat with her.

"I remember now. We have met before," Faye said. "You came to my door asking questions about my husband."

"You're the lady whose husband was just murdered?"

"Yes."

"I'm so sorry. Hillary told me about it. She knew him quite well."

"I know."

"The reason I was asking questions was that when Hillary found out about her illness, she wanted to leave half of everything to the older brother her parents had adopted out the year before she was born. I did some research and found out it was Hank. I'm sorry if you didn't know that, but he was the right age, and the only man in the community born in that month."

Faye realized that if it was true, it explained Hank and Hillary's sudden break up. Maybe Hillary didn't know that Hank was really her brother—he found out somehow and that's when the break up occurred. It seemed Hillary didn't find out until years later. "It must've been an awful shock for them."

"That's right, they had been dating. She told me that, but she had no idea. Now she knows why he ended their relationship. He must've found out."

Faye was right and Hillary must've been heartbroken and that drove her to set fire to his barn. Then Faye thought more about the likelihood that Hank had been adopted. His parents hadn't been married that long before he arrived. "I doubt you've got the right man. Hank can't have been adopted."

"He was."

She shook her head. "I can't see how it makes sense."

"I met with his stepmother, and she pretended she didn't know anything about it, but I found proof."

"What proof?"

"It's in the garage. Would you like to see it?"

"Yes." She followed him in, figuring she'd see perhaps a letter, or some kind of document.

When they were both in the garage, he pointed to a plastic carton. "Over there."

As she started walking toward it, she realized she'd seen him somewhere else too. He was the paramedic—the one who'd given her those pills the night her husband died. She whipped around to face him.

He had his two fists up and in between them was a cord. She tried to duck away, but he managed to slip it around her neck. He was pulling it tight— strangling her. *He's Hank's killer and tried to kill me that night.* She realized the tablets he'd given her weren't sleeping tablets; they were some kind of poison. It would've looked like she killed Hank and then poisoned herself. A nearly perfect crime, but she hadn't taken those pills.

She couldn't let him get away with it.

An image of her baby came into her mind and she knew she had to fight for her baby. Her hands went to her throat in an effort to loosen the cord. When that didn't work, she tossed and turned, trying to hit him or elbow him but she couldn't get at him. Her vision started going black and sparkly at the edges. Everything faded. In the distance, she thought she heard the siren of a police car, but it was going to be too late.

WHEN SHE OPENED HER EYES, she saw she was in bed surrounded by white. A familiar face appeared from out of nowhere and looked down at her. Was it Hank? Was she dead? A second later, she knew it was John and she knew she was alive. Her fingers went to her aching throat. It felt like it was on fire. She realized her neck was loosely wrapped in something cooling, and that seemed to be helping.

"Don't try to speak," he said.

She closed her eyes and the scene played out before her. Hillary's husband had tried to kill her. The pieces of the puzzle fell into place. Hank's murderer wasn't Silas, or John, or even Hillary. It was Hillary's husband.

Hillary was wealthy and searching for her brother. It seemed her husband didn't want to share her wealth with anyone else, so he had to murder Hank before Hillary died. Then when Faye hadn't died from those pills, he tried to kill her with bees in case Hillary's will wasn't changed before she died from the cancer. Bees would have looked like an accident, she figured. Then he laid low for a while before his next attempt on her life, and she had obligingly stepped right into his lair.

When she opened her eyes again, she saw Detective Hervey standing next to John. She told them about the pills and the paramedic.

"We have him in custody. We'll need you to testify about what he did to you."

She nodded as best she could. "My baby?" she asked in a croaky voice, reaching down to her belly.

"The baby's fine and the doctor said you are, too. They did an ultrasound to be sure. You just need to rest," John's deep voice reassured her.

The detective confirmed everything she'd already figured out. Except for the fact that Hank wasn't Hillary's adopted brother. "We did some checking and there was a baby boy adopted by an Amish family. He was born in the same year and month as your husband, but he died at two years of age from a fever."

"Oh, that's so sad," she whispered.

"Hillary's a very sick woman—terminally ill."

"I know." Then she heard a squeal. She looked over to see her mother hurrying toward her.

The detective stepped back. "Her husband also admitted to taking a knife from your house to kill your husband with. And we found those pills you told us about. If you'd taken them, you wouldn't have lasted the night. They were cyanide—a deadly poison."

A chill ran down her spine that someone—a killer—had been in her house and she'd never known. If she'd taken those sleeping pills, she would've died and her unborn child would've died along with her.

"I'll stop by again tomorrow, Mrs. Kirkdale."

"Thank you," John said to him.

"What happened, Faye?" Her mother scurried over to her.

John told her mother everything.

"Oh, you poor thing, Faye." Her mother leaned over and smoothed back her hair just as she used to do when she was a small child.

Faye closed her eyes.

"I'll go now," John said.

Faye raised her arm. *"Nee,* please stay."

"I'll stay as long as you want."

"Can I have water?"

He poured a glass of water and helped her sit up. After a couple of sips, she asked, "How did the police find me?"

"Hervey figured it out from what you told him. He went to your house and when you weren't there he knew you'd gone to confront Hillary and her husband. You shouldn't have gone there alone."

She nodded. She knew that now.

"You could've been killed."

"My *boppli* and I are safe."

"Your *vadder* is worried and waiting by the phone in the barn. I'll call him and tell him you're all right."

"*Jah,* I'm okay."

Her mother used the phone in the room to call her husband, and while she was busy, Faye turned to John. "How did you get here?"

"I had just arrived at your house when the detective pulled up. He told me where he thought you were and I went in the car with him."

If only her mother wasn't there, this would be a perfect time for him to ask her to marry him. Then her life would be complete.

Her mother placed the receiver down and stood between the two of them. "When will you be coming home?"

"I don't know."

"She'll be here overnight," John said, "and the doctor said she shouldn't speak too much."

"You'll have to come back and live with us, Faye."

"*Nee.* I've got my own home. The danger's gone."

"You always were a stubborn girl."

"Don't speak so much, Faye," John told her.

She closed her eyes, in no mood to listen to her mother's reprimands.

"Well, if you're not going to talk to me, I might as well go," her mother said.

"*Jah,* she'll be okay. I'll wait with her until she goes to sleep."

"*Denke,* John. I do have the boys at home."

"She'll be fine," John said.

Faye's mother leaned over and kissed her on the cheek. "Bye, for now. Call and let me know when they let you leave."

"*Jah, Mamm,*" Faye whispered. She watched her mother walk out the door, glad that she'd come, and now relieved that she had gone.

"The doctor said you'll be hoarse for a while, but the baby's just fine, so don't worry.," John said.

"That's all that matters."

"Is your throat sore?"

She nodded. "Hurts bad when I swallow."

"Try not to talk. *Gott* spared you. The doctor said a moment later and you would've died. I'll sit here with you for a while."

She nodded.

"Do you want me to wait until you fall asleep before I go?"

She nodded again and silently thanked God.

"It's nearly midnight. The nurses should be back to check on you soon."

She closed her eyes and hoped she'd feel better in the morning and then her life would get back to normal. Perhaps not normal, but at least she'd be free from the fear of being killed, since they'd arrested Hank's murderer.

WHEN SHE OPENED her eyes the next morning, the first thing she saw was John beside her, asleep in the chair. His head was leaning too far over to one side and Faye hoped he wouldn't wake with an ache in his neck. She pushed herself into a seated position and helped herself to water. It still hurt when she swallowed.

He woke up and smiled at her. "Good morning."

"Hello."

She couldn't believe that she had once suspected him of murdering Hank.

"How are you feeling?"

"I've been better."

He chuckled and then rubbed his neck.

"Denke for staying here."

"I had nothing better to do, since you won't let me near Hank's business."

"I might need some help. A little bit."

"I'll give you all the help you want. Now don't talk."

When a man in a white coat walked in the door, John said, "Here's your doctor. I'll wait outside."

He examined the wound around her throat and looked at her chart. "You'll be sore for a while, but you're all right to go home. I'll give you a script for some anti-inflammatory painkillers that are safe to use during pregnancy, and if anything changes for the worse I want you to go to your own doctor."

"I can go home?" she whispered.

"Yes. They've told you that your baby is unharmed?"

She nodded, a tear in her eye.

The doctor gently patted her hand and then left, and John came back into the room.

"I can go home."

"Good. I'll drive you."

"Can you call Rain and tell her …?"

"*Jah,* I will. I'll do that now."

JOHN DROVE her home and walked her inside.

"Faye, you're going to need someone to look after you."

Of course she would, and he was just the man to do it. She smiled at him, waiting for his marriage proposal.

"Can you stay with someone? Perhaps you could stay with your *mudder* for just a while. You look so pale."

Her heart sank. He meant look after her in the short term. "I'll feel much better here in my own home."

"Then I'll have no choice but to check on you every day. Please don't tell me you're going to work."

"I've been thinking about that. Perhaps I could use a little help."

"Really?"

She nodded.

"At last you see sense."

"I said 'a little.' I'll still be in charge, since it's my company."

He chuckled. "Now, what can I do for you before I go?"

Faye didn't want him to go at all. "I've got hardly any food in the house. Can I give you a grocery list and you take it to Rain?"

"I'll do it. I'll get it now."

"I can't—"

He held his hand up to shush her. "You can't talk, remember?"

She nodded. "Okay."

"Shh."

She giggled. And stopped short, because that hurt, too.

When she had written out the list, she handed it to him.

"*Denke*. It's times like these I miss my car. I could've zipped down and zipped back with the shopping. Now it's going to take half a day." He looked back at her and smiled. "I'll enjoy the ride with the fresh air in my face."

She nodded so she wouldn't get into trouble for speaking. When he left, she walked into the kitchen and took out the baby clothes from their hiding place. She looked at each piece in turn, imagining what her baby would look like. They hadn't said if this ultrasound had showed the baby's sex, and she didn't want to know.

BEFORE JOHN CAME BACK with her groceries, Rain arrived. Faye was pleased to see her friend, but had hoped to have more alone time with John.

Rain rushed in to see her and Faye told her, in as few words as possible, everything that had happened. Just like Faye had thought, Rain was still there when John came back with the food. Then he left soon after.

CHAPTER 12

For the next several weeks, Faye kept her distance from John as far as she could except at work. The John at work was all business and there was no conversation that was of a personal nature. She was having a baby and he was being integrated into the Amish. The day of his baptism, she thought she should say something. She was now at a point where everyone knew of her pregnancy as she was so large she couldn't conceal it.

"Hey, John."

"Hello, Faye. How have you been?"

"Good."

"Good."

It was an awkward start.

"I've been worried about you," he said. "I haven't been near you because I wanted to give you space."

"I figured that. I've been doing the same for you."

"Oh. Well, that's good."

"Good all 'round then." She smiled at their funny talk about nothing in particular.

"Have you thought about what's going to happen with work when you have the *boppli?*"

"I'll bring the *boppli* to work with me."

He frowned. "Is that being practical?"

"What do you suggest?"

"I suggest that I do more and you do less. I'll run every big decision past you. I know you don't want to give up control."

"I guess I could take a back seat for a few months, but I'd need to know everything that's happening."

"That seems like it would be best for you and everyone."

"We should talk more about that tomorrow," Faye said, not wanting to talk about business on a Sunday.

He nodded and she walked away. At least her mother had stepped back from trying to force her to have one of her brothers run the company, now that John was on the scene. Now Faye knew that John was interested in the business and not her. He'd had plenty of opportunity to express himself before now. If he hadn't proposed to her by now, he likely never would. There were so many single young women in the community and they outnumbered the men. He'd most likely choose one of them to settle down with. Seeing him at work every day while he was married to someone else would be hard.

A thought occurred to her. Perhaps he thought it was too soon after Hank's death. If she shared with him that she'd been forced into the marriage, maybe that would make a difference. That is, if he liked her in that way at all.

She glanced back at him and saw two young women approach him. Then she looked down at herself with a wry smile. Not many men would think of courting a widow who was heavy with child.

Then a funny thing happened. He looked around as though he was looking for someone, and when their eyes met, he smiled at her as though he'd been caught out. He was looking for her to see where she'd gone. At that moment, she knew for certain that he liked her. But if that was so, why wasn't he doing anything about it?

For the next several weeks, Faye had no choice but to exercise patience, which wasn't easy for her.

Patience awaiting the arrival of her baby and patience waiting for John to propose, or at the very least suggest they do something together outside of work.

With Rain's help and her mother's help, Faye had everything ready for the baby's arrival. As each day got closer to her due date, Faye got increasingly sadder that her baby wouldn't know its father and that Hank wouldn't ever hold his baby.

As Faye sat behind her desk in her office, her mind drifted to how her life might be different if Hank was still alive. Now, Hillary's husband awaited trial, and Hillary was pondering returning to the community for her remaining months. So much had changed in the past year, Faye mused, and now her life was completely different. Silas had moved away, which Faye was pleased about, and Faye had grown closer with Hank's step-mother.

Her baby was due any day now and Faye had to wonder why she was hanging on to Hank's business. John had offered to run it, so why didn't she let him? Perhaps it was because she didn't like to be told she couldn't do something. She'd proven she could run the company adequately, with help, yes, but still she ran it. Could it have been pride that made her insist on doing everything herself? She placed her hand over her stomach when she felt a kick, and knew the most important thing was her baby, more important than anything.

In that moment, she decided she would step back and allow others to do things. John could take on the top management position. He was doing most of the work anyway and she always turned to him now before making decisions.

"Good morning."

She looked up to see John. "Hello. I need to talk to you about something."

"Good. Me too. You go first."

He sat in front of her and she had a horrible thought. What if he was leaving? What if he was getting married to someone else?

"You go first," she said, holding her breath.

"*Nee,* you."

"You're not telling me you're leaving, are you?"

"Never. Okay, I'll go first." He looked around, then he jumped up and closed the door. "I've been doing a lot of thinking and praying."

"About what?"

"About you and your *boppli.*"

"Oh."

"I want your *boppli* to have a *vadder,* and someone needs to look after you. I was wondering if you might consider marrying me?"

153

She smiled. It was what she'd wanted for so long, but not quite the way she wanted it said. He mentioned nothing of his feelings for her. "Out of duty?"

"*Nee.*"

"You're doing me a favor?"

He gulped. "I would like us to marry. I would like very much to be married to you."

She wanted him to say he loved her, but what if he didn't feel that love? If she ever were to marry again, there would have to be love on both sides. "I will only marry again for love."

He looked down. "Oh, I'm sorry. I thought …"

"Thought what?"

"I didn't think, I hoped … I hoped you might feel something for me."

"I do, I do."

He looked up at her. "You feel something?"

Now she could see in his hopeful eyes that he loved her. "I do."

"Like?" He was smiling now.

"I do like you and perhaps a little more."

He rubbed his chin. "You love me?"

"I can't say that until …"

He walked around to her side of the desk. "Until what?"

She shook her head and a large lump formed in her throat. She couldn't speak.

"Faye, I've been so frightened to say how I feel about you. I want to be in your life, and I thought if I told you how I really feel, you'd reject me and feel awkward around me." He took a large breath and kneeled down in front of her. "I still want to be in your life as your friend if you reject me. I need to tell you that I love you and want more than anything for you to be my *fraa*. I want to be *vadder* to your child, not just *onkel*."

She needed to make sense of it all and wondered if he'd loved her years ago before he left the community. "When did you start feeling this way?"

"When I came back and saw you after Hank died, I knew I should've never left in the first place. I had a burning desire to make something of myself back then and didn't know what love was. I liked you back when I was a teenager, but never showed it. I thought nothing of love or how rare it was. Now that I have a chance with you, I don't want to let you go. Unless you don't feel the same. If you don't, I'll still be the best *onkel* your *boppli* will ever have."

Faye giggled. Today was possibly the best day of her life. "I have so many brothers, my *boppli* will have no shortage of *onkels*. What my *boppli* needs is a *vadder*."

He smiled. "And what do you need, or what do you want?"

"You."

"Really?" He took hold of her hand.

She held onto his hand, squeezing tight. Tears rolled down her cheeks as she nodded.

He leaned forward and with his free hand he wiped her tears away. "Will you marry me, Faye?"

"*Jah,* I will."

He kissed her on her forehead. *"Denke."*

A stabbing pain thrashed across Faye's lower abdomen. "Oh! The *boppli's* coming."

"Now?"

"Soon. I need to call the midwife."

"I'll do that for you and then drive you home."

As he fussed about looking for the midwife's number, Faye smiled. She had someone she loved to look after her and her baby, someone to love them.

EIGHTEEN HOURS LATER, Faye held her baby in her arms. Rain, Faye's mother, and the midwife gathered around as Faye looked down at the baby girl.

Faye had already told them the news about marrying John.

"What will you call her?" her mother asked.

"I don't know yet."

"Are you really marrying John?"

"*Jah,* I am."

"We'll get everything cleaned up so he can come in and see you," Rain said.

The midwife added, "The poor man must be exhausted after waiting downstairs all this time."

Faye thought that a weird thing to say. After all, she had been the one having all the agony and doing almost all of the work.

"When John comes in, can everyone leave us alone?"

Everyone agreed and minutes later, John walked into the room. "How are you?"

"Fine. Look at our little girl."

He stepped forward slowly. The baby opened her eyes. "Look at her. She's so beautiful." Tears filled his eyes.

"She is." Faye kissed her on the top of her bald head. "I can't believe she's finally here." She looked up at him. "Don't change your mind."

He chuckled. "I won't. I feel like I'm the most blessed man in the world. I'm back where I belong and I've got something I've always wanted, a wife and a child. We'll marry as soon as we can. When I leave here, I'll go to the bishop and make all the arrangements."

"Okay."

"Can I get you anything?"

She shook her head. "Everything I ever wanted is right here in this room."

He leaned forward and kissed her cheek. "I love you, Faye, and I love our child."

Faye knew he was going to treat her daughter as his very own. "Here, hold her. You pick a name for her."

"Me?" He carefully took the baby from Faye and cradled her in his arms.

She smiled at the sight. "*Jah,* you decide on her name. I'll have to like it, though."

"Of course. How about Faith? Faith in *Gott* brought me back to you and got me through hard times."

"I love it. Faith Kirkdale."

TWO MONTHS LATER, Faye and John married and moved into a new house so they could start afresh. Throughout the first year of their married life, Faye was involved in the business, but as their family grew over the next five years with two more children, a boy and then another girl, Faye was more content to stay at home. John came home every night in time to have dinner with them, and even after years of marriage he never stopped being attentive and loving. John was the husband that Faye had always hoped for and she thanked *Gott* every day.

Thank you for reading 'Amish Widow's Decision.' If you'd like to be notified of my new releases and special offers, add your email at the mailing section of my website:
www.samanthapriceauthor.com

Samantha Price

Book 16 Amish Widow's Trust is the next book in the series:

When Amish woman Rachel Kiem's husband dies in a fatal shooting, she's left pregnant and alone. Plagued with guilt for sending him to the convenience store where he was shot, Rachel does her best to adjust to life alone by focusing her attention on the birth of her baby.

The outpouring of sympathy from the broader community over her husband's senseless death causes the press to become obsessed over the expectant Amish widow and her life. The more she ignores the attention, the more they want to learn about her.

With Rachel worried about her baby, hiding from the prying eyes and concerned over the recent arrival of her wayward sister, will she miss a fleeting opportunity when an old flame comes to town?

OTHER BOOKS IN THE EXPECTANT
AMISH WIDOWS SERIES

Book 1 Amish Widow's Hope

Book 2 The Pregnant Amish Widow

Book 3 Amish Widow's Faith

Book 4 Their Son's Amish Baby

Book 5 Amish Widow's Proposal

Book 6 The Pregnant Amish Nanny

Book 7 A Pregnant Widow's Amish Vacation

Book 8 The Amish Firefighter's Widow

Book 9 Amish Widow's Secret

Book 10 The Middle-Aged Amish Widow

Book 11 Amish Widow's Escape

Book 12 Amish Widow's Christmas

Book 13 Amish Widow's New Hope

Book 14 Amish Widow's Story

Book 15 Amish Widow's Decision

Book 16 Amish Widow's Trust

Book 17 The Amish Potato Farmer's Widow

Book 18 Amish Widow's Tears

ABOUT SAMANTHA PRICE

A prolific author of Amish fiction, Samantha Price wrote stories from a young age, but it wasn't until later in life that she took up writing full time. Formally an artist, she exchanged her paintbrush for the computer and, many best-selling book series later, has never looked back.

Samantha is happiest on her computer lost in the world of her characters.

To date, Samantha has received several All Stars Awards; Harlequin has published her Amish Love Blooms series, and Amazon Studios have produced several of her books in audio.

Samantha is best known for the Ettie Smith Amish Mysteries series and the Expectant Amish Widows series.

To learn more about Samantha Price and her books visit:

www.samanthapriceauthor.com

∽

Samantha loves to hear from her readers. Connect with her at:

samanthaprice333@gmail.com

www.facebook.com/SamanthaPriceAuthor

Follow Samantha Price on BookBub

Twitter @ AmishRomance

43957312R00093

Made in the USA
Middletown, DE
01 May 2019